THE TORNADO

JAKE BURT

FEIWEL AND FRIENDS
NEW YORK

For Mom and Dad

A Feiwel and Friends Book
An imprint of Macmillan Publishing Group, LLC
120 Broadway, New York, NY 10271

Our books may be purchased in bulk for promotional, educational, or business use. Please contact
your local bookseller or the Macmillan Corporate and Premium Sales Department at
(800) 221-7945 ext. 5442 or by e-mail at MacmillanSpecialMarkets@macmillan.com.

Library of Congress Cataloging-in-Publication Data.

Names: Burt, Jake, author.
Title: The tornado / Jake Burt.
Description: First edition. | New York : Feiwel and Friends, 2019. | Summary:
    For Bell Kirby, school is about sketching and avoiding a bully who happens
    to be the principal's son, until new student Daelynn arrives and turns
    everything upside-down.
Identifiers: LCCN 2019001972 | ISBN 9781250168641 (hardcover) |
    ISBN 9781250168634 (ebook)
Subjects: | CYAC: Friendship—Fiction. | Bullying—Fiction. | Schools—Fiction. |
    Creative ability—Fiction. | Clubs—Fiction.
Classification: LCC PZ7.1.B887 Tor 2019 | DDC [Fic]—dc23
LC record available at https://lccn.loc.gov/2019001972

Book design by Sophie Erb
Feiwel and Friends logo designed by Filomena Tuosto

First edition, 2019

1 3 5 7 9 10 8 6 4 2

mackids.com

PROLOGUE

Servicechat.Army.Gov   **Connected**

All right, genius. You ready for the hardest father-son puzzle you've ever faced?

Yeah!

Took me all week to think this up. So far, it's stumped half of Wiesbaden.

Bring it.

Here goes. Uploading the image now.

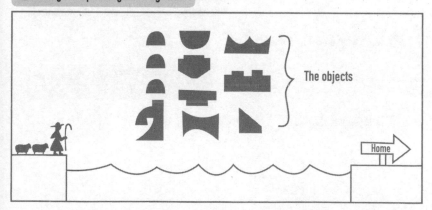

The objects

A shepherd, weary from protecting her flock from mountain lions, vicious tigers, and grizzly bears, dreams of finding a new home—one where her flock can graze safely. It's not a place she can reach by boat or by train; she has to make the journey on foot . . . and she's nearly there. Trouble is, she's reached a river, wide and deep and rushing. Fortunately, she's collected some objects on her journey—ones that might prove useful here. Can you use the objects to build a bridge for her and her sheep?

And there you have it, master engineer. Good luck . . . You're going to need it.

I like the little sheep.

Those are killer lemmings chasing her.

You're weird.

I know, right? I get it from my kid.

That's not how genetics works.

That's what makes it so weird!

I love you, Dad. Thanks for the puzzle. I'll look at it tomorrow.

Love you too. *Tschüß!*

CHAPTER ONE

Bell Kirby was *supposed* to be drawing a map of Central America. If any of his classmates had bothered to look, they'd have seen him hunched over his desk, scribbling furiously with a black pen. They'd never guess the curves weren't the borders of Honduras or Guatemala, or the straight lines weren't longitude, or that it wasn't even his social studies notebook hidden in the halo of his arms.

And that was just fine with Bell.

He needed all of silent work time to sketch and resketch those strange puzzle pieces his dad had sent. Was one of them a crown? A spinning top? A faucet? He paused, cracking his knuckles and rubbing his ink-stained palms together. All he had to do was concentrate a bit longer, and he was sure he'd have it. Not even Parker Hellickson could distract him—Bell was that zeroed in.

But then Daelynn Gower touched down in his classroom like a tornado.

The door burst open, and a backpack slid across the floor, spewing its contents everywhere: colored pencils, pink erasers, unicorn folders, a purple glasses case, and three mandarin oranges. A pair of green-handled lefty scissors spun dangerously close to Bell's foot, forcing him to lift his legs before his sneaker got skewered.

Just behind the backpack rushed a girl.

"I am *so* sorry! I forgot to re-zip after I got my glasses out, and I didn't know the door was going to open like that! I'll clean it up! Here!" the girl said as she scampered around. She chased an orange all the way up to Mrs. Vicker's desk, then veered toward Bell, leaning down to pick up her scissors. Blushing, he lunged over his notebook to hide what he had drawn . . .

And found himself staring into a rainbow.

The girl's hair was cut short, like a candy-coated cap, and it was dyed turquoise and yellow and magenta. Her glasses, as thick as the ones Bell used to wear before he got contacts, had blocky red rims. When she looked up at Bell, he stifled a gasp.

Her eyes were two different colors, too. The left was a regular shade of eyeball-blue. The right was startlingly green.

She smiled sheepishly at him, revealing two lines of braces, each one featuring a multicolored rubber band. Bell shifted silently in his seat. Inside, he was screaming at the girl to go away. Every second she was near him was a moment that Parker Hellickson was watching, too.

Clenching his teeth, Bell scooted her scissors forward with his toe until she found them and hurried back to the front of the classroom. He only exhaled once he saw that Parker's eyes were narrowed at the new arrival. Still, Bell curled up as small as he could at his desk, just in case, and he pulled a few locks of his shaggy blond hair down like a curtain for good measure.

"Class," Mrs. Vicker muttered after looking skyward and shaking her head. "This is the new student I was telling you about. She'll introduce herself in a moment. Can we remember who *we* are by helping her pick up the things she's dropped?"

A few kids closest to the front slid from their desks, scrounging on the floor for erasers and colored pencils. The girl opened her hands, but she couldn't hold everything, and a couple of erasers escaped to bounce underneath the nearby bookshelf.

"Thank you, Adrienne, Chris, and Zayne. And welcome . . ." Mrs. Vicker paused, checking a piece of paper on her desk. "Die-lynn?"

"It's 'Day,'" the girl replied, pushing up her glasses. "But that's okay. I get all kinds of different things. You can call me 'Dye' if you want. I guess I've got the hair for it."

Bell chuckled briefly, though he bit his lower lip and looked down at the floor when he saw that nobody else was laughing.

"And where was your old school, Daelynn?" Mrs. Vicker asked, hitting the "Day" particularly hard.

"There wasn't one," Daelynn said. "I did homeschooling."

Bell felt every muscle in his neck and back tense at once. He had to force himself to keep breathing. Daelynn rubbed nervously at the logo on the sleeve of her jacket. It looked to Bell like a deer, or maybe a moose. Underneath the jacket, she wore a T-shirt with several anime characters drawn across the front. Her pants were covered in patches, and the one on her left knee seemed to be a flower of some sort. The right knee patch was another of the moose things, just as colorful and shocking as her eyes.

Is this how homeschooled kids dress? he thought.

At least her bright red sneakers looked kind of normal.

Mrs. Vicker cleared her throat. "And where was home?"

"Portland, Oregon."

Bell's teacher nodded appreciatively. "Portland! That's a long way from Cincinnati!"

"Yes, ma'am," Daelynn replied, "and we drove."

"Well, welcome to Village Green Elementary, home of the Pioneers!"

Daelynn smiled, and Mrs. Vicker led her through a few more questions. Bell contemplated opening his notebook again—normally, he'd have spent the entire class with his head hovering a few inches from its pages, pretending to take notes while he drew. This Daelynn, though, was hard to ignore. And it wasn't just the colors, or her breathless entrance, or the homeschooling, or her laugh, which ended just like the last flutters of air squeaking out of a balloon.

4

She was a new variable in his system, kind of like when they moved the snack table inside for morning recess. It jammed everyone up at the same double doors, especially on chocolate-chip granola bar days. It took Bell three weeks to redesign his route outside, and he'd been tripped and teased and had his granola bar stolen a half dozen times as he tried to figure it out. That had been a bad time.

And, based on the scene Daelynn had made when she came in, this had the potential to be much, much worse.

CHAPTER TWO

After homeroom on Thursdays, the fifth-grade classes split up for specials. Some of them had computer. Bell had music. So did Parker Hellickson, which meant getting out of class safely was a tricky proposition. The way it was *supposed* to go looked like this:

- Bell drops one of his pens at 8:56.
- Bell leans down to get it at 8:57 and uses the opportunity to untie his left shoe.
- Mrs. Vicker hands out graded homework at 8:58.
- Homeroom ends at 9:00.
- Bell waits forty-five seconds, tying his left shoe while the rest of the class leaves.
- Bell approaches Mrs. Vicker to ask about his homework at 9:01.
- Mrs. Vicker explains how to do the problems

6

(he always makes sure to get at least one wrong).

• Bell exits the classroom at 9:03, giving Parker enough time to have cleared out of the hallway.

• Bell takes his special route to music, avoiding Parker and arriving with five seconds to spare.

Things most certainly did not go that way, though. Bell was so distracted that he forgot to drop his pen, and he had to tie his shoe twice to cover the forty-five seconds. Worse, when he went to ask Mrs. Vicker about the homework, Daelynn and Ashi Sadiq were there already.

"You sure you don't mind helping Daelynn find her way around today, Ashi?" Mrs. Vicker asked.

"Nope!" Ashi replied, and then she turned to Daelynn. "I like your patchy pants!"

"Thanks," Daelynn replied. "I like your earrings!"

Ashi giggled. "Yeah. My dad got them for me at Union Terminal. They're dragonflies."

Mrs. Vicker interrupted, "Did they give you a schedule this morning, Daelynn?"

Daelynn glanced at the pile of papers under her desk. "There were lots of forms. Hold on."

Bell tried to slip in as Daelynn went to rummage, but

Mrs. Vicker shook her head. Bell looked at the clock and then his wristwatch.

"I've got . . . um . . . music," Daelynn said, looking down at a crumpled sheet.

"Bad luck," Ashi sighed. "I've got computer. But I can meet you after."

Daelynn's shoulders slumped, and she glanced nervously at the door. Mrs. Vicker pursed her lips for a moment, but then her eyes widened and she slid her glasses to the very end of her nose.

"Bell Kirby!" she said cheerily.

"Finally," he replied, and he stepped between Ashi and Daelynn, slapping his spelling homework down in the usual spot on Mrs. Vicker's desk, right between the sticky notes and her WRITE MAKES RIGHT mug. She slid it back to him.

"No, Bell. We don't have time today. Or rather, you don't, because you're going to help Daelynn get to music. You *do* have music now, don't you?"

"But the homewo—"

"You'll figure it out just like always, Bell. Go on now."

Daelynn looked at Bell, who pulled the hood of his gray sweatshirt up and tugged the drawstring tight.

"Oh, he doesn't have to, Mrs. Vicker," she said. "I . . . I can ask someone on the way."

"Bell would be delighted to assist," Mrs. Vicker countered. "He's offering."

Bell raised a finger to object, but it wilted under his teacher's stern gaze.

"See you back here for math, kids. And Daelynn, it was lovely to meet you," Mrs. Vicker said, and she waited while Bell grabbed his notebook and backpack and shuffled out into the hallway . . .

A full minute too soon.

The banks of lockers on either side of Mrs. Vicker's classroom door made a little alcove for Bell to hide in, which he did. Still, it wasn't much, and Ashi was chatting loudly with Daelynn right behind him. He gritted his teeth as he stole a peek at his wristwatch.

9:02 and thirty-eight seconds.

A sheen of sweat had broken out on Bell's brow, which he wiped away with his sleeve. He flicked his tongue back and forth under the sharp ridge of his chipped incisor, and he pulled his hood back so he could listen down the hallway better.

"Well, bye, Daelynn! Enjoy music," Ashi said.

"Shhh," Bell whispered, but the girls ignored him.

"Thanks . . . Ashi?"

"Yep!" Ashi replied, and she hurried off to computer.

9:02 and fifty-one seconds.

Bell took a deep breath, ready to exhale when he was in the clear. Daelynn, though, tapped him on the shoulder. His quiet sigh of relief turned into a terrified squeal, and he cast his head left and right.

A few passing kids snickered, but there was no sign of Parker Hellickson.

Disaster averted.

For now.

"I'm okay," he whispered.

Daelynn stared at him. He couldn't even look back; her different-colored eyes were too intense.

"Um," Bell managed eventually, "music is down the hall, then left, then up the stairs. It's the second door on the right."

"Aren't you going, too?" Daelynn asked skeptically.

"Yeah," Bell said. "But I . . . I don't go that way."

"Oh. Okay," Daelynn replied. "I guess we can go your way. I'm ready whenever you are. And thank you."

"No," Bell replied sharply. She flinched, and Bell held up his hands. "I mean, no, sorry. No problem," he said, and turning so fast his sneakers squeaked, he marched stiffly down the hall, arms crossed over his notebook. Daelynn scampered to catch up, scratching the turquoise side of her head in confusion.

Bell stopped right where the staircase led up to music class. With Daelynn watching, he was sorely tempted to take the regular way. But he knew Parker sometimes lingered at the top of the stairs, and if he saw Bell with Daelynn and her patchy pants, eerie eyes, and electric hair?

That was a risk Bell couldn't take.

Instead, he turned right, skittering down the opposite staircase. Daelynn hustled behind him, all the way through the gym, into the kindergarten wing, and then up the back stairs to the third floor. At the door into the hall, Bell stopped, poking his head past the doorframe to see if the coast was clear.

"What are you looking for?" Daelynn asked.

Bell ignored her.

"I . . . um . . . like your way to music. It's . . . twisty?"

A group of kids burst from the bathroom across from the music room. Parker was among them, laughing as he bent Justin Dwyer's fingers back in a game of mercy. Justin was whimpering, but he was giggling, too. Bell spun, hiding behind the doorframe. Of course, that brought him face-to-face with Daelynn. He swallowed and looked down at his shoes.

"Hey, do you have any pets?" Daelynn said.

Bell's face screwed up. "What?"

"Nothing." Daelynn shrugged, kicking at the floor with her red sneakers. "It's just that this morning, my dad told me that if things got awkward, it's good to ask other kids about their pets. He said it was an icebreaker. Sorry."

Bell's shoulders slumped. He knew awkward pretty well, and she was right.

This was most definitely awkward.

He turned around again. Parker had gone into the music room, and the hallway was empty. With a shiver, Bell crept forward. He heard Daelynn sigh behind him, and he paused.

"What?"

"I just noticed your notebook. Did we need one for music? Because I don't have—"

"It's not for music," Bell said, and he tucked it tighter under his armpit.

"Oh! Is it a sketchbook?"

"No!" Bell snapped, and she apologized softly.

More awkward.

"I have a chinchilla," he murmured.

"What?" Daelynn gasped.

Bell cringed.

"A chinchilla," he replied. "It's kind of like a rabbit, only—"

"I know what chinchillas are!" Daelynn chirped. "I love them! They're so furry and cute! Like chubby squirrels."

"Fuzzgig is not a chubby squirrel," Bell protested.

"Its name is Fuzzgig?!" Daelynn practically shouted. "Like Fizzgig, from *The Dark Crystal*? I love that movie!"

"I . . . uh . . . yeah, actually," Bell said. He blinked rapidly. She was the first kid he'd ever told about Fuzzgig who got the reference.

"That's so cool," she said.

Bell nodded. "Thanks . . . but you can't be that loud in the hall," he whispered.

"Oh, I didn't know . . . There wasn't a list of rules in the packet they gave me. Is . . . is there a list of rules?" she said, looking around like she expected to see a grand scroll of the Village Green Elementary guidelines posted on the wall somewhere.

"Not really. Maybe in some of the classrooms. They're usually up at the front, near the board," Bell replied, and he looked at his watch.

They had arrived at the music room at 9:04 and fifty-six seconds.

Despite the unexpected disruptions, his system had worked.

Barely.

CHAPTER THREE

Bell hurried past the substitute music teacher, who was too busy fiddling with the DVD player to look up. When he reached his usual stool at the back of the room, his first peek was at Parker, who was in turn watching Daelynn. She stood at the doorway quietly. The longer the substitute ignored her, the more nervous Bell got. Mrs. Vicker had made him responsible for her, after all. He tried to clear his throat, at least, but he lost his nerve when Parker barked, "Hey, sub!"

The man turned around, adjusting his belt and straightening his too-short tie.

"It's Mr. Warner," he said. "And I'll be with you as soon as I get this thing working . . ."

Parker jerked a thumb toward Daelynn. "The new kid is staring at you."

Mr. Warner jumped when he saw Daelynn. She gave him a little wave and blushed.

"Oh, yeah. Plans mentioned a new girl. Uh . . . go on up there and have a seat next to that other guy. I'll take attendance in a second."

Mr. Warner pointed to an empty stool, and the entire class turned to look. Bell's head shrank down into the hood of his sweatshirt. The stool was right next to him. As Daelynn ascended the low, broad steps that made up the student section of the room, Parker watched her like a hawk. And when she sat down, his gaze snapped over to Bell.

Parker grinned.

Bell gulped, and he quickly cast his eyes downward, huddling over his notebook. He opened it and used it to shield his face even more.

In addition to being his only hiding place at the moment, Bell's notebook was his pride and joy, proof of his love for and skill with systems. There were pages and pages of them, whether it was the step-by-step instructions for getting from homeroom to music without crossing Parker's path, or the long, unbroken blueprint that dominated the margins—a million-part machine designed to take a plate of cookies he drew on page one all the way to the crumb-munching crocodile he sketched on the inside of the back cover. There were fulcrums and forklifts, catapults and corkscrews, elevators and slides. Interspersed along the way were power sources: generators, rivers, solar panels, and the occasional chinchilla on a wheel. Everything was connected—a perfect plan to get the cookies to that crocodile.

So far, they had made it to page ninety-nine, out of two hundred.

Bell would have loved to have continued his drawing of the massive machine, or to keep working on his dad's puzzle, but he had adjustments to make back on page twelve, so he leafed through, only half raising his hand when the substitute called out, "Joseph Kirby?"

Daelynn tugged lightly on his sleeve, startling him. "Is that you? Are you supposed to say 'here'?"

He wriggled his arm away from her and raised it high. "Here!" he announced.

"Joseph? What happened to Bell?"

"It's my middle name," Bell whispered, and he buried his eyes back in his notebook.

At the top of page twelve, the heading read, "Thursday Mornings, Homeroom to Music." On the bottom of the page, he had drawn three cranes with hooks at the ends of their ropes, designed, of course, to carry the cookies across to page thirteen. Above, there was a flowchart, branching and crossing itself like a spider's web. In the bubbles, which Bell liked to imagine as bugs caught in the web, were questions, the answers to which were written in tiny letters along the arrows that led away from each bubble. The very first question read, "Is Parker in school today?" Depending on the answer, the chart would lead to more questions and more possibilities: "Did Parker go to the bathroom during homeroom? If yes, then take route number four. If no, refer to table seven-B." On the opposite page, just next to a cookie-flinging slingshot, was an intricate graph that featured every single student's class schedule, cross-referenced with their between-class habits. Parker, for instance, if he hadn't already gone, stopped to use the bathroom between homeroom and music 21 percent of the time. When he did, he used the second-floor boys' bathroom 98 percent of the time. And regardless of whether he went into the bathroom or not, he got a drink of water 83 percent of the time.

Even Bell would acknowledge that this was a bit excessive. But he had his reasons . . . Like his chipped tooth, for instance.

Or, he thought as he snuck a glance at Daelynn, the specter of homeschooling.

CHAPTER FOUR

It was September of his fourth-grade year, a few months before Bell had perfected his drinking fountain approach. They had just finished playing ultimate Frisbee at recess, and it was still hot enough outside that Bell had a good sweat going. Most kids crammed their way toward the crummy trickle machine just outside the gym, standing in a long line for the privilege of playing germ roulette at Village Green's most frequented and least effective water fountain. Bell knew better, though. He scampered down the hall toward the cafeteria and the brand-new fountain, the one powerful enough to fill water bottles and cold enough to make his eyes cross.

With no line in front of him and no one behind, Bell was free to take his time. He closed his eyes tight, so that his sweat couldn't drip down his forehead and sting him, and he let the jet of water cool his tongue, rattle his teeth, and drench his chin. Imagining he was overcoming some end boss's ice ray, he gradually lowered his lips. It didn't matter that he was only managing to drink about a quarter of the water—it felt *good*. So good, in fact, that he was utterly unaware of the boy sneaking up behind him.

Bell had to admit that Parker's timing was perfect; had his face been any farther from the fountain, Bell's teeth wouldn't have crashed into the metal spit guard when Parker smacked the back of his head. But Parker had waited until just the right moment, and so Bell's incisor collided with the stainless steel, an audible *ping* accompanying the sudden sensation of ice-cold water jetting up Bell's nose. By the time Bell had recovered enough to feel the throbbing in his jaw and the rapid ballooning of his upper lip, Parker was well down the hallway, laughing and scooting out of sight.

Bell tried to retreat to the bathroom to check out the damage, but Ms. Copely, the art teacher, heard him sputtering and sniffling. She marched him straight to the nurse's office for an ice pack, then to the principal to relay his story. Bell protested as best he could with a Ziploc bag full of ice cubes shoved against his mouth, but it didn't do much good. She left him right outside the office doors, where the words MR. HELLICKSON—PRINCIPAL were frosted across the glass in big, blocky letters.

Parker's dad welcomed him in, offering him a tissue and a wide grin. It took Bell a full five minutes to tell his story, what with the mixture of lip blood, melty ice, and stifled-sob-snot he had to swallow every few seconds. It was as he was clenching his teeth to keep from full-on crying that he felt the sharp stab on his tongue: his right incisor had been fractured, leaving it with a decidedly vampiric point. He reached in with a finger to test the edge of it just as Mr. Hellickson called Parker's teacher.

Bell sat up as straight as he could and dabbed at his eyes, determined not to show Parker his tears. The other boy sauntered in a few minutes later, grabbing a butterscotch from the dish on his dad's desk and popping it into his mouth. Mr. Hellickson smiled, but when he saw how hard Bell was staring at him, he took a deep breath, rubbed his fingers along his mustache, and cleared his throat.

"Parker, son—Bell here tells me you might have accidentally run into him at the drinking fountain. Is that true?"

Parker looked at Bell, his face unreadable . . . at least, for the moment. Then his eyes opened, wide and unblinking—just long enough for a glint of moisture to form at the corners.

"I . . . maybe, Dad? I was in such a hurry to get to class! I think . . . I might have bumped him? I'm really sorry if I did, Bell!"

Another wave of fresh, angry tears welled in Bell, and his words got twisted as he fought them back.

"It wasn't . . . no accident . . . my mouth . . ."

"I appreciate your honesty, Parker," Mr. Hellickson said. "It's a shame about your tooth, Bell. I'll have to call your mom and let her know what happened here; maybe she can

20

get a dentist to do something for you. Until then, you should try to calm down. Best to keep a stiff upper lip."

Parker put a hand over his mouth to hide a smirk as Bell wilted. Mr. Hellickson seemed oblivious.

"And before you go, Bell, I think you should thank Parker for the apology. After all, you know a little something about accidents, am I right?"

Bell grimaced. He knew exactly what Mr. Hellickson was talking about.

Parker and Bell used to be . . . well, not exactly friends, but playdate acquaintances? They both lived on the same street—Bell in a little place near the top of the quiet hill, Parker in the massive house at the bottom. Through second grade, their parents had brought them together every so often. Parker would come over to play Bell's video games. Bell would get dropped off to swim in Parker's backyard pool, or to shoot at Parker's soccer goal. Every single one of those "games" ended with Bell losing a gigajillion to nothing, mostly because Bell got bored after the first five minutes and let Parker score to keep him happy. Then, though, on one muddy Saturday in April, Bell decided to try out the "slide tackle" thing Parker had been telling him about.

He slid . . .

He tackled . . .

And Parker ended up missing the U8 Elite Invitational Final with a broken big toe.

Bell wore his voice out apologizing, but it didn't help.

21

Soccer was pretty much Parker's life, and when he couldn't play for a couple of months, revenge was his replacement. That's when Parker got *mean*: honest-to-badness, make-fun-of-your-family, steal-stuff-from-your-cubby, jab-fingers-in-your-ribs-type bullying.

And when Parker found out he could make other people laugh? That he could win favor with his soccer buddies at Bell's expense?

Well, that was game over.

Bell had talked with his parents about it. Oh, *gosh*, had he talked to his parents about it. Night after night in fourth grade . . . bedtime reading turned into "What did Parker do today?" venting sessions. They had theorized about the whys: It made Parker feel in control? It got him attention? It kept him at the top of the social ladder? It filled some void in Parker's life? All of his mom's psychological reasons made sense, Bell supposed, but they didn't much help. And they had tried all the strategies, from "kill 'em with kindness" to "join in the joking—make fun of yourself!"

Bell's mom had even gone in to talk to Mr. Hellickson.

Eight times.

After that eighth meeting, she had come home, found Bell in the garage, and taken him out to Graeter's for wild cherry ice cream sodas. Over a mountain of whipped cream, she said, "Bell, your father and I have been chatting, and we think you've suffered enough. How would you feel about pulling out of school?"

Bell nearly choked on a maraschino.

"You're making me drop out?!"

Bell's mom slid a hand across the table, touching his arm.

"The army's giving me a sabbatical next year while I start on my Ph.D. My schedule would be flexible enough that I could homeschool you."

Bell lost his appetite. He wasn't sure why the thought of homeschooling terrified him so much—after all, he wouldn't be around Parker every day. But there were things he loved about school, too: His classes. Creator Club. Timmy.

Mostly, though, he was afraid of starting something different. Of *being* different.

So he adopted one final strategy: supreme avoidance. No contact with Parker meant no trips to Mr. Hellickson's office and no calls to Mom, which meant no more conversations about homeschooling. Hence his systems—"Thursday Mornings, Homeroom to Music" had managed to get Bell safely from first to second period for his entire fifth-grade year so far. However, none of his plans accounted for Daelynn Gower.

Bell dared a glance at her over the edge of his notebook. She was looking around wide-eyed, staring at the cartoony posters of musical notes with faces and marching tubas with legs. It was like she'd never been in a music classroom before . . . which, Bell realized, she probably hadn't.

Yep. It was definitely time for some revisions.

CHAPTER FIVE

When the movie started, most of the kids found subtle ways to ignore it. Some whipped out Sharpies and started doodling on their shoes. A few did homework for other classes. Bell worked on his notebook, mumbling to himself as he crossed out several threads of his flowchart. Then he began drawing a slow, straight line through the narrow passage between bubbles . . .

. . . which promptly became a lightning-bolt zigzag when a whisper nearly scared him off his stool.

"I love this movie!" Daelynn sighed. "It's my favorite of, like, all time!"

Bell glared at her. She had scooted her stool forward, and she seemed to be transfixed to the TV screen as the sepia clouds rolled behind the opening credits of *The Wizard of Oz*. To the rest of the class, this was nothing to celebrate. Their music teacher, Ms. Ollivant, was pregnant, and had no problem requesting days off. "If I'm going to war with the eight-pound kick-demon in my belly for the entire semester," she had declared on the first day back after winter break, "I'm declaring at least a day or two a week as an armistice."

At first, the kids had loved the idea of a sub every few days, but they soured on it quickly once they realized that Ms. Ollivant left the same plan every single time. Since the substitute was never the same person twice, he or she didn't know where the movie had left off, and so whoever it was just started the whole thing over again, no matter how much the kids protested—the sub plans were very specific, apparently. It wouldn't be long before the entire class had those first thirty minutes memorized.

And Daelynn, it seemed, was ahead of the curve.

Every time Bell tried to sink into his system, she'd murmur a quote from the movie, pulling his attention back up. Other kids stared at her, too. The way she swayed along with the songs and shifted on her stool was more entertaining than the movie. And Bell found himself snickering on occasion, too; Daelynn did a mean Zeke impression, and when she wagged her finger at the TV and said, "Listen, kid, are you going to let that old Gulch heifer try and buffalo you?" it had Bell forgetting about his notebook for a second and laughing out loud.

So loudly, in fact, that it caught Parker's attention.

Generally, Bell felt safe in class while the teacher was there; Parker was too smart to do anything where he might get caught. But a substitute made things less sure, and with a wild card like Daelynn in the mix, all bets were off. Whispering to friends, for instance—if it was Mrs. Vicker, she'd squash that conversation like a bug. But the sub was busy reading a newspaper, and so he didn't notice Parker talking to Tam and Justin. He also didn't notice the way that Parker jerked his head back toward Bell.

Bell noticed, though.

Frantically, he skipped to the section of his notebook labeled "Contingencies." Marching along the left side of the page was a perfect row of "ifs":

- If there's a fire drill . . .
- If Creator Club is canceled . . .
- If I'm paired in group work with Parker . . .

And so forth. Near the middle of the page, Bell spotted what he was looking for. "If Parker is going to trap you after a special . . ." He ran his fingers across the words to reassure himself, and then he shot out of his seat. He could feel Parker's eyes on him as he skirted the classroom on his way to Ms. Ollivant's desk. The substitute glanced up from the sudoku he had almost finished.

"Can I go to the nurse?" Bell whispered.

Mr. Warner glanced at the clock. "What's the matter?"

"Headache," Bell lied.

"Not going to puke, are you?"

Bell blushed. "I don't think so."

Mr. Warner sighed. "Then you can wait two minutes for the class to be over. Tell your homeroom teacher about your head. I'm sure whoever it is will let you go."

Bell gritted his teeth. He'd have to come up with another plan: "If Parker is going to trap you after a special AND there's a sub . . ."

For now, though, Bell was forced to slink back to his stool, hoping for a miracle in the next two minutes.

CHAPTER SIX

Two minutes.

Zero miracles.

"So we only get to see the first half hour?" Daelynn pouted when the substitute dismissed them.

Bell nibbled a fingernail, his face twisting as he tasted the ink on his fingertips.

"Bell?"

"What? Oh, yeah. That's it."

"Guess we should get back to Mrs. Vicker's room for math, yeah?"

Bell didn't look at her. He was too busy watching the clock. Parker lingered by the door, his mouth so close to Justin's ear as he whispered that it seemed like he might bite it. A prickle ran up Bell's spine.

Parker never stuck around this late after class.

"Um . . . Bell?" Daelynn muttered. "Should I try to get back on my own?"

Bell blinked, then cast around. He spotted Kai North, another kid in Mrs. Vicker's class.

"Follow him. He'll get you back."

"You're not coming?"

Bell shook his head rapidly. Daelynn waited a couple of seconds more, but when it became clear that she had to choose between following Kai and not getting anywhere at all, she shrugged and scampered off. Bell didn't notice—he was too nauseated just thinking about what he'd face outside those doors. And the sub wasn't going to be of any help: one glance revealed Mr. Warner poking at the DVD player and cursing under his breath. Still, as Bell stepped into the hallway, he had to hope his fears were all in his mind.

Nope.

Definitely not just in his mind.

Parker leaned against the bulletin board outside the music room door, chatting with Justin, Tam, and Shipman. As soon as Bell came out, Parker clapped once and sprang forward. Bell tried to get past as fast as possible, but Parker was faster, and Bell felt the rubber toe of Parker's shoe jam against the back of his ankle. Bell's notebook went flying out of his grip, and his knees cracked painfully on the floor as he went down.

Parker's buddies laughed.

Bell loved formulas and equations, but bully math was a different story. Even though Parker Hellickson was universally mean, he still had dozens of friends. Bell, who tried to be nice as much as possible, had one, or maybe two, if Parker wasn't around to influence people. That's why, when Parker flat-tired him, there were three people there to scoff at Bell, but none to help him up.

"Dropped your notebook," Parker said lightly as he watched Bell scramble to retrieve it. Justin, Tam, and Shipman slouched behind him.

"Th-thanks," Bell muttered.

"Dude gets tripped, and he says thanks," Justin observed, and they laughed again. Bell winced, but he didn't try to run. That only made it worse. And besides, since Parker had stepped right up into his face, he had Bell pinned.

Bell wasn't that much shorter than Parker. In fact, they were about the same size, though Parker's AAU soccer practices had him carrying more muscle. He had a narrow, clever face, curly brown hair, and a mole on his neck that always had two hairs poking out from the top. But it wasn't Parker's size that scared Bell so much, or his face, or the mole. It was the kid's willingness to do just about anything, at any time, to anyone. Immediately, Bell went into Parker Protocol:

- Stay still.
- Answer in short words.
- Stare at the mole, not the eyes.
- Don't ignore him.
- Don't fight back.
- Don't call out for help.

"See anything worth mentioning in music class, Bell?" Parker hissed. The other guys around him just stood there smiling, except for Tam, who was messing with the zipper of his jacket.

"No."

"You sure? Saw you looking at the new girl. She's really weird, eh, Bell?"

"She's fine."

"Fine? Like, normal fine, or *fine*?"

A laugh from Justin and Shipman. Tam rolled his eyes.

"Normal fine."

"Uh-huh," Parker said, and he casually lifted his hand to his nose, shoving his middle finger into his left nostril and rooting around. He didn't get much, but what he did he proceeded to drag out, regard appreciatively, and then wipe on the cover of Bell's notebook. The color drained from Bell's face.

"Dude, that's nasty!" Shipman said, his eyes sparkling.

"Oh, gross!" Justin agreed, and he clapped Parker on the shoulder. Parker chortled, then leaned in. Bell flinched.

"Think she hates you yet, Bell? Like everyone else?"

Bell's hands squeezed his notebook so tight they went numb, even with the smear of nose juice down the center. He clenched his jaw as Parker started rolling through all his old standbys—jokes about Bell's mom and dad, mostly, and other things that had upset Bell in the past. Before Parker could come up with any new material, though, the substitute teacher stepped out into the hallway.

31

"Boys getting back to class?" Mr. Warner asked, his arms crossed.

"Yes," Bell said woodenly, and he marched off as quickly as possible, taking advantage of every second of teacher-observed time to get out of Parker's field of vision. When he was free, he bolted back to Mrs. Vicker's classroom, reaching it well before Parker and his friends strolled around the corner. Safely inside, Bell set his notebook down. The spiraled spine had left a perfect pattern on his palm. He grabbed a tissue, squirted some hand sanitizer on it, and scrubbed Parker's snot off, grumbling to himself as he did. The truth was, even though he didn't cry, all Parker's old jabs still hurt: every single one of them. At least he was safe here, he thought, and there was only . . .

Ugh. Five hours to go until Creator Club.

Most of that time, Bell couldn't stop watching Daelynn. To someone not as keenly interested in the way things were supposed to work, it might have seemed like she was doing okay for her first day. But to Bell, she was equal parts fascinating and agonizing. It didn't seem to bother her at all that she was dressed so differently from everyone else. At the same time, she fidgeted in her seat like a kindergartner, she had to ask dozens of questions, and she didn't even know how to use the electric pencil sharpener. Worse, whenever Mrs. Vicker gave her anything, she wouldn't put it away. Instead, Daelynn kept all the papers and books in a halo around her, as if she were afraid her desk would swallow anything she put in there. It was all Bell could do to keep from jumping up, stacking her materials in a neat little pile for her, and running off before Parker could make fun of him for helping her. In fact, Bell felt himself get angrier and angrier at her, until even the completely normal things she did made his skin crawl.

But then came read-aloud, and Daelynn twisted his perceptions yet again.

At two fifteen, Mrs. Vicker solemnly put her dry-erase marker down. Instantly, students slapped their writing notebooks shut, shoving them into their desks. A great shuffling filled the room as many students retrieved scrap paper. Some sighed happily and sank their heads into the crooks of their arms. Others, like Parker and Tam, slipped out of their seats entirely, jostling each other as they jockeyed for position on the big pillows at the back of the room.

Bell brought his precious notebook out and hovered over it like a dragon guarding its hoard.

Daelynn looked mystified. Her hand shot up.

"Oh, yes," Mrs. Vicker said as she settled into her wicker rocking chair in the corner. "Can someone explain to Daelynn what's happening?"

Ashi volunteered.

"At two fifteen every day, we have read-aloud. You can draw, you can rest your eyes, or you can grab a book and read along," she explained, pointing at a row of copies of *Island of the Blue Dolphins*, "but you have to be quiet, and you have to listen."

"I can draw?" Daelynn echoed slowly. Mrs. Vicker

nodded, and Daelynn's whole face lit up. Her hands shaking, she reached into her desk and retrieved a sketchbook. She slid it forward, arranged it just so, and then opened it as Mrs. Vicker began to read. Stunned, Bell watched as Daelynn leaned over that book, her arms crowding its edges. She gripped a colored pencil so tightly her knuckles turned white, and she seemed to lose herself in the pages below her.

Bell blinked, momentarily forgetting about his own notebook. How was it possible that a new girl, one with rainbow-spiked hair and a mile-wide mess around her ankles, could suddenly look so very much like him?

CHAPTER SEVEN

Bell's garage was, in his estimation, the most wonderful place in the world. The Creator Club room ranked a close second, though.

For starters, Parker wasn't in Creator Club. Add that to the fact that Timmy Korver, Bell's best friend, was, and it was already rock-solid as far as he was concerned. Throw in the most awesome teacher at Village Green Elementary School, and it was a recipe for greatness.

And that's without even mentioning the room itself.

Bell felt like he was shrugging off five tons of tension when he hung his backpack on the hook by the door. Smiling, he ran his thumbs along his temples, brushing his hair back behind his ears as he breathed in the familiar scent of the room. It smelled of sawdust and wood glue, applesauce and felt-tipped pens. Every wall was covered in shelves, and on every shelf was pure potential: unopened packs of graph paper, the cellophane wrappers glistening. Rows of pencils that had only been sharpened once, each one the exact same size as the one next to it. Fuzzy pipe cleaners, utterly unbent. Popsicle sticks and toothpicks in perfect stacks. Paper clips that had never been mangled into makeshift lockpicks. Modeling clay and Play-Doh that were still soft.

There were even boxes of markers that contained every color.

And they had all their caps.

Kids had already filtered in, grabbed snacks from the counter, and sat at the brightly colored workbenches— benches they had built themselves at the start of the year. Bell's team had decorated theirs in a dinosaur motif. On the seat at Bell's end, he had painted a styracosaurus, its spiky-crested head lowered in warning. At the opposite end was an ankylosaur, its own heavy, hammer-like tail lifted into a guarded position. And in the middle? A pack of velociraptors, clawing and crawling all over the seat.

At the moment, though, none of the velociraptors were visible. Timmy Korver's torn-up track pants made sure of that.

"Buuuh!" Timmy blurted, applesauce spattering the paper that covered the table. He had been slurping his snack without a spoon, the plastic container of applesauce held between his lips while he sucked the sauce through his teeth like a strainer. Timmy bowed his head, placing the cup on the table. There was still a glob of applesauce on his nose.

"Nice to see you, too," Bell said, grinning. He was fluent

enough in saucespeak to recognize his own name when he heard it.

Timmy scooched over, exposing a velociraptor. Bell joined him, his notebook placed well out of applesauce range.

"It's today, Bell!" Timmy proclaimed, drumming his hands on the table.

"Seriously?" Bell said. "You actually heard Mr. Randolph say that?"

Timmy coughed.

"Well, no. But he's been hinting at it for the last three weeks."

A heavy bag thumped onto the end of the table before Bell could reply. The Nike logo, along with the faint smell of grass and feet, told the boys that the third member of their bench team had arrived. Like Bell and his notebook, Nhan-Tam Nguyen rarely went anywhere without his cleats, and had Mrs. Vicker not told him he had to leave them in his locker, he probably would have lugged that bag to every class, plus lunch.

"Hey, Tam! Today's the day!" Timmy said.

Tam put down the tower of applesauce cups he had taken and shrugged.

"Okay?"

"The Creator Contest? Mr. Randolph has to give us the guidelines today!"

"Okay," Tam repeated, tearing the foil off the topmost cup in his stack.

"Hey, Tam," Bell said.

Tam shoved a spoonful of applesauce into his mouth, then swallowed.

"Hey, Bell. Sorry about Parker."

Timmy growled. "What did Hellickson do this time? And do I need to stomp him for you, Bell?"

Bell looked down at his feet. "Don't worry about it, Timmy."

Tam nodded. "Listen to him. Getting in a fight with Parker would be the dumbest thing you could possibly do. First"—Tam paused, glancing up and down at Timmy—"you're even smaller than Bell."

"Parker won't touch me. He's too afraid of my older brothers."

"I wish I had two high school football players looking out for me," Bell muttered.

"Three!" Timmy said proudly. "Alan made varsity!"

Tam waved his hand. "None of that even matters . . ."

"Yeah, yeah," Timmy sighed, running a finger along the inside of his applesauce cup to pick up the last sugary ribbons, "Parker's dad is the principal. I'd get suspended for so long I'd be able to drive myself back to school. I get it. But why are you friends with him if you know he's such a jerk?"

Tam glanced at Bell, then looked away. "He's on my soccer team. And he's funny sometimes, I guess."

"But you're Bell's friend, too!"

Tam shrugged, and he ended the conversation with

another mouthful of applesauce. Bell nudged Timmy with his shoulder.

"It's all right. Besides, if your prediction is correct, we're going to have better things to think about than Parker Hellickson."

"Or new kids in class," Tam murmured.

"Hey!" Timmy said. "That's right! You got a new kid! I hear she's weird."

Timmy was in the other fifth-grade homeroom. They mixed and matched between the two for specials like music, art, and gym, but depending on which classes they had on a given day, Bell might not see Timmy at all, and Timmy had to rely on lunch and Creator Club for inside information.

"I don't know. She's definitely . . ." Bell paused. He was going to say *strange*, but he thought again about the way she'd leapt into her notebook at read-aloud. "Interesting. She has dyed hair. And she was homeschooled . . ."

"I wonder what that was like," Timmy said.

Bell shuddered. "I have no idea," he replied quickly.

"She's nuts about horses, too," Tam added.

"Horses?"

"Yeah. She's in my art class. As soon as Ms. Copely asked her what she liked to draw, she started this ten-minute speech about horses. I guess they used to own some before moving here. Anyway, yeah, horses."

Bell thought he recalled seeing a horse patch on her pants.

"She's funny, I guess," Bell added. "She knows all the words to *The Wizard of Oz* and can do the voices pretty well."

Timmy smiled. "If she knows that much about *The Wizard of Oz*, she'll fit right in. At least, she's all caught up in music class."

Bell nodded, and he reached for an applesauce off the top of Tam's tower. He pulled his hand back, though, when Mr. Randolph arrived.

"I don't care if it's cups or cleats, construction paper or cardboard castles. Clear your tables!" the man boomed. To a one, every kid bolted to obey, flinging applesauce cups into the trash, putting half-done projects on shelves, and scampering back to their seats. It wasn't that they were scared of Mr. Randolph, though he was twice even Tam's size. No, they just knew that when their Creator Club teacher arrived, *something* awesome was bound to happen.

Today, it seemed, would be no exception.

Mr. Randolph had tucked under his arm a sheaf of papers, rolled up and tied together with a string. This he set down on his desk with great ceremony. His huge hands dwarfed the pair of scissors he picked up, and it seemed a strange thing to see so impressive a man make such a dainty cut of that string. When he did, the papers partially unfurled. Over these Mr. Randolph leaned, his long, gray-streaked beard hanging far enough to dust the pages beneath him.

"To me, creators," he said, softer this time. It didn't have any less of an effect. The students swarmed his desk, with Bell, Timmy, and Tam crowding at the corner.

Mr. Randolph was one of the smartest people Bell knew, maybe even as smart as his mom. He had three Ph.D.s—one from Louisiana State University, one from Grambling State University, and one from the University of Cincinnati. The diplomas were displayed prominently on the wall behind his desk, even though he could have put them in his office at UC. He was a professor there but volunteered at Village Green every Thursday to run Creator Club. He told the kids that the reason he kept his diplomas at their school was that he had nothing to prove to the people at the college, but "Kids? They can smell a fake a hundred miles off. You want to teach a fifth grader, you better bring your credentials."

"Ladies and gentlemen," Mr. Randolph rumbled. "I bring to you this year's Creator Contest challenges . . ."

"Yes!" Timmy whispered. "Called it!"

Bell ignored him. His eyes were riveted on those papers.

"They come to you from another time, creators. Another place. In fact, you might say we'll be dabbling in the occult. After all, we will be attempting to channel the spirit of one of the greatest inventors in history . . ."

Mr. Randolph slid his hands across the roll of papers, finally flattening them so the sixteen students crowded around could see. On the first sheet was a sketch, well weathered, of a naked man, trapped in both a circle and a square. His limbs had been drawn twice, so that he appeared to have four arms and four legs, and he was surrounded by tightly written words in a language none of them could decipher. Bell recognized the drawing immediately.

"Leonardo da Vinci!" he exclaimed.

"Just so, Bell," Mr. Randolph said proudly.

"That's Leonardo da Vinci?" Timmy asked. "Why's he all naked?"

Tam shot Timmy a look. "He's got extra arms and legs, and you're worried about his clothes?"

Mr. Randolph laughed deep and long. "No, Timmy, Tam. This is one of da Vinci's most famous sketches. He was a renowned artist during the Renaissance in Italy, 'round about the same time Gutenberg was printing his Bible, England was fighting the Wars of the Roses, and Columbus was sailing the ocean blue. You've probably heard of the *Mona Lisa*?"

Everyone nodded.

"That was da Vinci. But he was so much more. He was a genius in many, many fields."

"Kind of like you?" asked Tessa Waumbach.

"That's sweet, Tessa, but I've got no qualms admitting that Mr. da Vinci has me beat, hands down. For instance, check this top drawing. It's an anatomical study. Does anyone know what that means?"

Timmy raised his hand.

"It's got the word *atom* in there . . . was he drawing what they thought atoms looked like back then? Maybe like, you know, tiny little people that joined together by grabbing each other's arms and legs? The elements that stuck together more, like oxygen—they'd have more arms and legs to grab other atoms. Like this dude here. He could grab eight other atoms—four with his fingers, and the others could hold on to his legs. That'd make him oxygen, because its anatomic number is eight."

"It's just 'atomic number,' and that's . . ." Mr. Randolph stared at Timmy for a second. "Wrong, but brilliant, Mr. Korver. I love the way you think."

Timmy beamed.

Bell said, "Anatomy is the study of the human body."

Mr. Randolph nodded, snapped his fingers, and then interlaced them over his tie.

"Nail on the head, Bell. Da Vinci was fascinated by the human body, and his illustrations helped advance the study of medicine. But he also made contributions to astronomy, history, botany, and, most important for our purposes . . ."

"Engineering!" five kids chimed at once.

"Engineering," Mr. Randolph echoed, and he slid the anatomical drawing out of the way, revealing the rest of the stack. Bell and his classmates broke into chatter immediately, pointing and grabbing at the sheets. Mr. Randolph slammed a palm down onto the middle of the drawings, and the room fell silent.

"Yes, these are your guidelines for the Creator Contest this year, but they're only general. Next week, each bench group will receive the plans for one of da Vinci's inventions, along with all his sketches and notes about the subject. Either using the materials we have here, or what you can find at home, you're going to attempt to make a working model of the invention you see on the paper."

"Can we work outside of Creator Club?" Bell asked.

Mr. Randolph chuckled. "Could I stop you?"

Bell smiled. Mr. Randolph knew him well.

"If you want to meet up on the weekends to work with your bench partners, that's fine. I will be asking for written progress reports, though, and I don't want to read anything about one kid taking over the project and not letting the others participate . . ."

Mr. Randolph peered over the rims of his glasses at Bell, who sheepishly looked away.

Maybe Mr. Randolph knew him *too* well.

Tam raised his hand.

"Mr. Randolph, if we have all the notes and the designs, where is the challenge?"

The teacher grinned, his teeth flashing as bright as his eyes.

"So, so glad you asked, Mr. Nguyen. First, it's true, you're going to get all of da Vinci's notes . . . just as he wrote them."

Mr. Randolph slid over to his desk. He tugged on the squeaky left drawer, and from it produced a heavy, blue-covered book, the dust jacket for which had long been torn away. Mr. Randolph cracked it open, licked his right thumb, and leafed through until he found a page bearing an illustration of what looked like a huge crossbow. Then he thumped the book down in front of Tam.

"What is this? Like, Italian?"

"Precisely, Tam."

Tam shrugged. "Fine. I'll just use the internet to—"

"Fifteenth-century Italian, in da Vinci's handscript. Oh, and he wrote everything backward, too."

"Why?" Timmy asked.

"Some folks say it was to protect his trade secrets, but I think it was just quicker for him. He was a lefty, you see," Mr. Randolph responded, holding up his left hand and wiggling his fingers. It made Bell think about Daelynn and her scissors.

"Still, I bet you could Google it," Tessa said.

"Oh, you could, but then you'd be cheating."

"Huh?"

"That's the other part of the challenge . . . ," Mr. Randolph said slowly, that big grin returning.

"Uh-oh," Timmy groaned.

"Here it comes," Bell added.

"You had to ask, Tam," Rachel Smith teased.

After a deep breath, Mr. Randolph declared, "In the construction of your projects, you will have access to any and all tools, resources, and references that you can think to use . . ."

Bell and Timmy high-fived.

". . . as long as da Vinci would have had access to them as well."

Timmy's and Bell's jaws dropped.

"That's right," Mr. Randolph said, his voice gleeful. "No Google, Tessa. No internet, period, Tam."

"No glue guns . . . ," Timmy whispered.

"No battery motors . . . ," Bell said.

"No 3-D printer . . . ," Tam whined.

"Mr. Randolph, will you still use the table saw for us?" Rachel asked hopefully.

He laughed. "I marvel at what da Vinci could have accomplished if he'd had the electricity to run a table saw! Or if he had a 3-D printer! But no, creators. None of that."

"What *can* we use, then?" Timmy asked.

Mr. Randolph reached out and tapped the top of Timmy's head. "Going to have to figure that one out yourself, Mr. Korver."

"Can we use the internet to research da Vinci, at least?" Tam asked.

Mr. Randolph rolled his eyes. "Let's say no, Mr. Nguyen. Try doing it the old-fashioned way. You know—with books? I know that's a stretch for your young minds, but it's one you better make soon: When we get together next, I give you your team designs, and the Creator Contest officially begins."

A half dozen hands went up with more questions, but Bell's wasn't one of them. He was already thinking about the familiar, welcome tingle in his fingertips. This *was* going to be a challenge, and he couldn't wait to get home to tell his mom about it . . . especially since, with this news, she might be too excited to ask him about everything else that happened today.

CHAPTER EIGHT

With his notebook tucked under one arm and the contest guidelines clutched in his hands, Bell set out from the Village Green Elementary parking lot. It was Cincinnati-January cold, the damp kind that snuck into his bones and took thirty minutes' worth of hot shower to shake. Bell hardly felt it, though. He was still too jazzed up from Creator Club. He watched his shoes glide over the bits of gravel and glass along the sidewalk. They felt like they wanted to sprint, to get him home as fast as possible so he could tell his mom all about the contest. But today was Thursday. That meant no indoor soccer for Parker, which meant Bell had to take the long way home. He stopped, still looking at his feet, and took a deep breath to remind himself to follow the system, no matter how excited he was.

"Hey! Bell!" someone shouted, and he could hear the slapping of sneakers on the sidewalk behind him. Red Converse All Stars, it turned out.

Bell looked up slowly, past the patchy pants, the kid-wizard on her anime shirt, and up to those green and blue eyes. He blinked rapidly; it was like each part of Daelynn was so unique that it took him a few seconds to put them all together into one person.

"Oh," she said, glancing around. "I don't mean to bother you. I . . . I just wanted to say thanks for this morning. Without you and Ashi, I'd probably be lost in the stairwell or something."

"What?" Bell asked. He was still staring at Daelynn's eyes.

She blinked, which snapped Bell out of it.

"It's called heterochromia," she explained, blushing. "Don't worry. I'm not a witch or anything."

"Sorry," he replied. "For, you know . . ."

Daelynn smiled. "It's okay. I get it a lot. That's why I wear these pants. Keeps people from staring at my eyes."

Bell couldn't help but look down at her pants again. She wiggled her left knee, making the horse patch flex and fold. "Just kidding, but made you look! Not that you wouldn't have. You look at the ground a lot."

Bell shrugged. He *did* keep his head down, after all. It was part of the system.

Daelynn stood there, red shoe tapping nervously while Bell watched. Then she blurted, "You should look up more often. Better chance of making friends that way. That's what my dad says."

Bell arched an eyebrow. She winced. Maybe she thought she had insulted him?

"And a greater chance of tripping," Bell countered.

She grinned. "You can see more smiles looking up."

"I see more four-leaf clovers looking down."

Daelynn narrowed those heterochromatic eyes of hers. "Might walk into a pole by looking down."

"Might step in dog poop looking up."

"More rainbows in the sky."

"More money on the ground."

"Less likely to get abducted by flying monkeys if you can see them coming."

"I . . . huh?" Bell murmured.

"Got you there," said Daelynn.

Bell could only laugh. "You're as bad as Timmy."

"Timmy?"

"Friend of mine. We're in Creator Club together."

"Is that why you're coming out late? I have to wait for my dad to pick me up."

Bell nodded, then showed Daelynn the paper he still clutched in his hands.

"Da Vinci! Ooh . . . I love his line style . . . Can I have this to show—"

"No," Bell said abruptly. "I . . . I've got to get going. Have a good afternoon. Or evening. Or whatever."

Spinning on his heel, Bell marched away from her as quickly as he could, leaving her to shout, "Thanks anyway!

Creator Club sounds cool! Um . . . Say hi to Fuzzgig for me!" He flinched and pulled up his hood, hoping the two boys who had just popped out of the main school doors hadn't seen him talking to her. Justin and Shipman weren't Parker-bad, but they were bad enough, and if they reported back to Parker that they had seen Bell talking to Daelynn . . .

Bell practically sprinted home, which normally would've only taken a few minutes. Village Green was just three blocks from the hill, and when Parker was at soccer, Bell could walk straight up to his house. Thursdays, though, took Bell all the way around to the backside of the hill—up, then over, then around the water tower, then home.

By the time he got to his house, Bell's ears were numb and his nose was running. He burst through the front door, slamming it so hard behind him that the stained-glass panels rattled. Then he took a deep, lung-stretching breath, letting the familiar smell of his house banish all the stress of the day.

There really was no place like home. Would it be the same if he had to think of it as school, too?

Once he had recovered, Bell kicked his shoes off, one flying into the kitchen. He followed it but didn't pick it up. Instead, he sock-skidded along the linoleum until he got to the door out to the garage. After jamming his feet into his thick-soled work boots, he stumbled through the door and yelled, "Mom!"

The light was on, but the garage was empty. Or, at least,

his mom wasn't there. It was otherwise quite full: Full of smells. Full of metal. Full of memories. Bell took a moment to close his eyes, inhaling the slight garlicky tang of acetylene, the grass-and-gasoline scent of the old lawn mower . . . and chocolate. When he looked around, Bell spotted his mom's heavy mug on the corner of her drafting table. The spoon still sat inside. Bell smiled and wrapped his frozen fingers around the blue ceramic. It was warm, and like always, his mom had left him the best part. He had already slurped up three scoopfuls of hot cocoa sludge when he heard her voice from the kitchen.

"Hey, buddy!" she called. "Um, shoes on the floor?"

"I'll get them in a sec, Mom. C'mere!"

Bell put his notebook down and hid the da Vinci paper behind his back. His mom stomped into the garage, her blowtorch in one hand and a mallet in the other. Her heavy goggles, hair up in two tight buns on her head, and the neon green safety mask she wore made her look like a bug-eyed alien. Bell twitched briefly, thinking back to after music class; Parker had discovered early on that jabs at Bell's mom were particularly good ways to get at him. But she put her tools down on the table and took off the mask, and her smile reminded him of the good stuff that had happened today.

"See you found the cocoa cup."

"Yeah. Thanks, Mom."

"Always my pleasure. You know it gets too sweet for me down at the bottom anyway," she said, leaning against the wall. Bell shuffled his feet to keep her from seeing behind his back. She squinted at him, and he snickered.

"Something you want to tell me, Bell? School today go well?"

"I guess," he replied.

"Any trouble with Parker?"

Bell's face scrunched up. "Not anything major," he stammered. "But we got a new girl in class!"

He had meant to tell her about Creator Club. Why had Daelynn suddenly popped into his head?

"Oh, really? Is she behind your back right now?"

"No!" he exclaimed.

"Ah. I see," Mrs. Kirby said slowly, reaching up to unpin her hair. It was blond like Bell's, and when she shook it out, it just barely tickled her shoulders. "Is she nice?"

"She's got yellow hair."

"Like ours?"

"No, like *yellow*. Neon."

"Huh. Cool!"

"And light blue."

"Cooler!"

"And magenta."

"Sounds like she's comfortable in her own skin. Good for her! If I had shown up for the first day of basic training with hair like that, they'd have turned me away!"

Bell smiled. It was hard to imagine his mom taking orders from a drill sergeant or climbing wooden walls in the pouring rain like they showed in movies, but her workshop shoes were combat boots, and he knew how disciplined she could be. Dad liked to say she had earned every single medal on her way to major twice over, and that he would have taken her into combat in a heartbeat. Mom always replied that she was perfectly happy in the Army Corps of Engineers, and with fighting the banks of the Ohio River when it flooded, rather than actual people.

"Yeah, yeah. She's okay," Bell said, pointedly avoiding any mention of her homeschooling. "Ask me what else happened at school today."

Bell caught a glimpse of his mom's mischievous grin as she turned away, idly scanning the massive collection of tools that dominated the closest wall of the garage. As a present for his parents last Christmas, Bell had cleaned up, categorized, and hung all his mom's tools, from the tiniest wrench to the heaviest hammer. His mom said it put most hardware stores to shame. Bell shifted from foot to foot.

"Mom, c'mon. Ask—"

"Did anything else happen at school today?" Mrs. Kirby murmured as she pretended to examine a Phillips-head screwdriver.

"We got the Creator Contest info!" Bell blurted, and he couldn't help but jump up and down, his heavy boots clomping on the concrete floor.

"Gimme!" his mom said, making grabby hands at the paper. Bell handed it over, and Mrs. Kirby, her own combat boots as loud as Bell's, snatched it and skipped to her light table. That had been Bell's dad's gift to her, an adjustable surface that was lit from beneath. The light would come through blueprints, making them much clearer to see, especially if they were layered on top of each other, like if someone was designing a two-story house. Or, in his mom's case, the structural plans for a dual-level bridge. Bell's favorite thing to do was stick his hand on it. It got so bright he could see all the bones and veins beneath his skin. It was awesome. Now, though . . .

"No, Mom! Wait!" Bell gasped, and he swatted her hand away from the light table's switch.

"Bell, what—"

"Candles!" he demanded. "Where are our candles?"

Mrs. Kirby arched an eyebrow. "Um . . . are you trying to burn down our garage again?"

"No!" Bell said, blushing. His second-grade Superpowered S'more Steamer hadn't done *that* much damage . . .

Mrs. Kirby tapped her foot and glanced at the ceiling.

Okay, so maybe there were a few burnt chunks of graham cracker still lodged up there, but the marshmallow had come off the walls easily enough.

"They're underneath the bathroom sink. Plastic bin."

"Don't touch anything 'til I'm back!" Bell shouted, and he took off.

Admittedly, the chemical aroma of acetylene didn't mix well with lavender, vanilla, cinnamon, pumpkin spice, ocean mist, or holiday pine, but scented candles were all they had. Bell arranged them around the edges of the light table, and his mom insisted on lighting them with her blowtorch, which she had affectionately named Sir Weldmore. Once the cloud of smells had settled around them (and she had put on her safety mask again, to survive the stench), Bell pulled his shirt over his nose and unfolded the sheet.

"We're going to build one of Leonardo da Vinci's designs, Mom!" Bell said, though with his nose covered, it came out more like "Deodardo da Dindi."

"Out of scented wax?" she replied. "That will be a challenge!"

"No," Bell laughed. "Out of wood, just like he would have. And that's why the candles . . ."

"Because the challenge is to do it Renaissance style . . . Nice . . ." Mrs. Kirby rubbed her hands together, and Bell could tell she was grinning even with the mask on. She spread the paper out, candlelight casting its glow along the little examples of da Vinci's artwork bordering the page of instructions. Mrs. Kirby hummed appreciatively and then nodded.

"So which one of these is yours?"

"Don't know," Bell admitted. "We find out next week."

"And how much time do we have?"

"It's due the week after the Spring Festival, so three months."

"No float building for you this year?"

"I don't think so," Bell replied. He had never joined any

of the groups who built floats for the festival parade, mostly because nobody had ever invited him. He told himself it was because he was always too busy with Creator Club, which made it hurt a little less.

"And Timmy and Tam are on board?"

"Timmy for sure. Tam's going to see if he can make it on Saturday evenings."

Mrs. Kirby took off her mask and blew out the candles one by one. Even though it was cold outside, she turned on the venting fans. Bell returned to the warmth of the kitchen.

When his mom joined him, he asked, "So, think it's doable?"

"Well, your father won't be on leave until mid-May, so we'll definitely have the space free. I'll see if we can't hit the library after work tomorrow to do a little old-fashioned research into what kind of tools we can use. You and your buddies finish that list of materials—I know you've probably already broken it down in that brain of yours," she said, rubbing her hand in Bell's hair until he swatted her off. "And then, next weekend . . ."

Bell's eyes widened, and he crossed his fingers.

"Next weekend, we'll hit the scrapyard."

"Yes!" Bell shouted, and he pinned his mom to the refrigerator with a hug. While the other fifth graders would be spending weekends watching TV, or sledding, or getting dragged to their sisters' dance recitals, Bell Kirby would be creating—just as he liked it.

After dinner, he rushed up to his room, notebook and da

Vinci instructions in tow. He was so excited to start researching that he nearly forgot to say hello to Fuzzgig, who scurried through his habitat excitedly as soon as Bell turned the light on. Once Bell had set his stuff down on his desk, he reached up to poke a finger into one of Fuzzgig's rooms, scritching the chinchilla behind the ear. He got an affectionate nip on the knuckle in reply.

"Hey, buddy," Bell said. "How was exploring today?"

Fuzzgig responded by jetting around the room, a feat made possible by Bell's engineering expertise. His greatest system, Fuzzgig's "cage," was actually a labyrinth of clear PVC tubes that ran along the walls, up the edge of Bell's bunk bed, across his ceiling, and to no fewer than seven bigger "playrooms," all filled with wheels, blocks to chew on, platforms to leap from, and hay to eat. There was even a glass sphere attached that contained Fuzzgig's lava dust, so that he could roll around and take what amounted to a chinchilla's bath. Bell's mom complained that Fuzzgig got more space in Bell's room than he did.

And she was right.

Once Bell sat in his chair, the chinchilla settled his gray, furry little self in the section of piping that ran along the back of the desk so he could watch what Bell was doing (and discern whether it involved giving Fuzzgig a raisin). Bell grabbed his pencil box, preparing to copy the instructions into his notebook so that he could make observations in the margins. Before he could draw the first letter, though, his gaze settled on the streaky spot where he had rubbed hand sanitizer. His shoulders slumped.

"That's right," Bell murmured. "Daelynn."

Fuzzgig tilted his head to the side, whiskers twitching.

"New girl at school," Bell explained. "You'd like her. She loves chinchillas, and her hair would probably be fun to chew on. It's all spiky and colorful."

If Fuzzgig was impressed, it was tough to tell. Bell sighed and flipped his notebook open to the next blank page. Rather than making notes about da Vinci, he penciled in what he could remember of Daelynn's schedule, then started cross-referencing it with his other charts. With the Creator Contest beginning, he needed Parker's attention anywhere but on him, and avoiding Daelynn seemed to be the best way to do it.

Of course, had he known what was going to happen the next week, he would have realized how hard that was going to be.

Servicechat.Army.Gov **Connected**

How was your day?

It was okay.

That great, eh?

Yep.

Any progress on the puzzle?

I wish.

Ha! The Great Bell Kirby—stumped!

Not stumped. Just haven't had time.

Well, if you have a chance, give it another look. And if you've got questions, I might have answers.

Thanks, Dad. I will.

Oh, one more thing before you go, Bell.

Yes?

Tell ur mom I think she's cute.

Gross!

LOL . . . JK.

. . .

But srsly tho . . . she's cute.

Ew.

Love you, Bell. Sleep well!

Love you too, Dad.

CHAPTER NINE

For his seventh birthday, Bell's parents gave him a plane ticket to Orlando, Florida. At first he panicked, thinking they meant to send him away for dismantling his mom's blow-dryer or for shoving french fries into the electric pencil sharpener to try to make potato soup. But then they revealed that it was because the family was going to Disney World over winter break, and Bell's terror turned to joy. After all, winter break was only a couple of months away . . .

And Bell thought he'd just about die after the first day of waiting.

Somehow, though, those two months seemed easier than the week leading up to the next Creator Club. First, there was the hype: everybody gossiping about which one of da Vinci's designs each group would get. Tam was holding out for the flying machine. Bell hoped for da Vinci's model of a clock, with all its moving parts and gears. Timmy wanted the giant crossbow.

Second, Bell couldn't seem to shake Daelynn. Sure, she was in his homeroom and music, and there was no avoiding her then. But if she wasn't with Ashi, she was pestering Bell about something or other—asking about Fuzzgig, or to see his notebook, or for directions to all sorts of places in school. For that, he couldn't really blame her; Village Green was three stories of brick and marble, and they had recently renovated it, too, so that it had doubled in size. The old school, with its sketchy staircases and rattling heaters, was buried in the middle of all the new stuff: dry-erase tables, open floor plans, and flat-screen TVs in the halls that played clips of the holiday assembly and announced what was for lunch each day. A new kid could get lost in a hurry.

Daelynn always seemed to be able to find him, though, which was why he wanted so desperately to get to Creator Club—it was a guaranteed Daelynn-free zone.

Or so he thought.

"Students!" Mr. Randolph bellowed as he made his appearance. Water bottles thudded onto tabletops. Whispers ceased.

A dozen kids swiveled on their benches simultaneously.

Mr. Randolph dominated the doorway, a briefcase in his hands. Bell noticed immediately that their teacher had handcuffed himself to the case, just like spies did on TV.

"Cool," Timmy murmured.

"I have your designs!" Mr. Randolph declared, and he hoisted the briefcase above his head. The chain of the cuffs dangled, glinting in the light.

The students scooted forward on their seats. Bell had to remind himself to breathe.

"But first . . . ," Mr. Randolph said slowly. "We welcome our newest member. Ladies and gentlemen of Creator Club, say hello to Ms. Daelynn Gower!"

Bell's eyes went wide, and his jaw locked tight. When Mr. Randolph stepped in, Daelynn was revealed. She looked around the room, and when she spotted Bell, she gave him a rapid little wave. His nostrils flared.

"Daelynn here will be joining one of your teams for the Creator Contest. You will make her feel welcome and catch her up to speed on the rules. Daelynn—please head to the bench shared by . . ."

"Not our team . . . not our team . . . ," Bell whispered.

". . . Ms. Smith and Mr. Wood!"

Rachel and Chris stood up, beckoning her to their bench. Timmy leaned toward Bell.

"Don't look so relieved."

Bell swallowed. "I . . ."

"We already have three. What are you worried about?"

"Nothing. I just didn't want . . ."

"A tryhard on our team? I get it," Tam said, turning back around to watch Mr. Randolph march up to his desk.

"What's a tryhard?" Timmy asked.

Tam pointed under the table at Daelynn. She was shaking her teammates' hands, asking them how they were doing and complimenting them on the colors they'd used to paint their workbenches.

"That's a tryhard."

Timmy scrunched his nose. "Oh, superhelpful. You should work for the dictionary company, with all that fine explaining you just did."

Bell poked both of them, then tilted his head toward Mr. Randolph. He had produced a silver key from his pocket, and he was ceremoniously unlocking the handcuff. Once he had it off, he made a show of rubbing his wrist. Then he flicked out his fingers like a magician preparing to produce a rabbit, and he unlatched the briefcase.

The room got silent again. Even Daelynn said nothing.

"Behold," Mr. Randolph commanded, and he used both hands to reach in.

They were scrolls, each one made of a fine, thick paper. Mr. Randolph, or someone, had used the old lemon-juice-and-a-lighter trick to make the sheets look old, and he had tied them closed with bits of glossy black ribbon. There were five in all, one for each of the Creator Club teams. The students applauded.

Walking table to table, Mr. Randolph laid a single scroll in front of each team. It was agony for Bell to watch the other benches get their plans first, because it was like Mr. Randolph was setting off private fireworks displays for the kids who got their designs—they opened them slowly, teasing those ribbons apart like the bows on birthday presents. Then they leaned over the plans, eyes wide as they pointed and ooohed. The first team got the ornithopter, which was basically a superfancy glider. Daelynn, Rachel, and Chris received a musical instrument called the viola organista. Bell's bench was last, and by the time Mr. Randolph got there, Timmy and Bell were bouncing up and down. Tam cracked his knuckles.

"And I've saved the toughest one for you, boys," Mr. Randolph said. "Observe: Leonardo da Vinci's tank!"

Timmy snagged the scroll. Tam swiped it from him before he could rip it open with his teeth, though. Carefully, Tam unfurled the page and laid it flat. All three boys stood, their heads so close they nearly bumped.

"Whoa," said Bell.

"That's a tank? It looks like a UFO!" Timmy observed.

"Or the top of a lighthouse," Tam added. "But with cannons coming out every side."

"Or the crappy popcorn maker my aunt got us last Christmas!" Timmy replied. "With firepower!"

Bell was barely listening. He was already enchanted.

This was why he loved systems so much: to him, there was a poetry in how things fit, whether it was moments rolling together into a schedule to get him from math to recess under Parker's nose, the way long division problems grew like vines down the middle of a page, or even the various mechanisms working together inside a toilet tank every time it flushed. To Bell, the broad, cone-shaped shell of da Vinci's tank was less popcorn maker and more a series of overlapped planks, cleverly tapered to interlock perfectly. The lower half, where presumably the drivers sat, broke down into four heavily spoked wheels. Bell smiled as he saw the interplay between those spokes and a set of gears, which were in turn connected to long crankshafts. His brain instinctively supplied the power source: people, turning those cranks to spin the wheels. Yes, the tank was a war machine, but it was gorgeous. It was elegant. It was . . .

. . . wrong?

Bell snapped out of his thoughts with a grimace. Mr. Randolph chuckled; he had been looking at his wristwatch. "Twenty-eight seconds, Bell. I had predicted thirty, and you beat me by a whole two ticks."

"Sir?" Bell said.

"I knew you'd detect the quirk quickly. Just didn't think it'd be that quick!"

"Quirk?" Timmy asked.

"Quirk," Bell replied. "Da Vinci's design has a mistake . . ."

Mr. Randolph wagged his finger. "Ah, Bell . . . don't be so quick to judge one of the greatest minds in human history! There's a design flaw, to be sure, but what if that was da Vinci's intent?"

"Where's the mistake?" Timmy wondered.

"Design flaw," Mr. Randolph corrected.

"Here," Bell said, and he pointed at the diagram of the lower half of the tank. "See the crank that turns the gears?"

"Yeah, right between the wheels," Timmy replied.

"Notice the position of the gears as they're set against the wheels?"

Timmy nodded.

"You spin that shaft, and it'll turn the gears. Then the gears turn the wheels by catching onto the spokes coming out of them. Trouble is, the gears are touching the inner halves of both wheels. If you turn the crank, it'll spin the front wheel backward and the back wheel forward. They'll fight against each other with the exact same push, which means . . ."

"Which means it'll go nowhere fast," Tam grumbled.

Mr. Randolph nodded. "You've got the idea, boys."

Bell ran a hand through a few of his cowlicks. "Why would he mess it up, though?"

"Yes," Mr. Randolph mused, "why would a man who dedicated himself to the study of life, knowledge, and beauty design a deadly machine of war that didn't work?"

"Ooh," Bell murmured.

"Oh!" Timmy exclaimed, and his hand shot in the air.

"It was a rhetorical question," Tam said, and Timmy put his hand down.

"Might be that it's the same reason old Mr. Randolph is going to tell you boys not to bother with the cannons on this one. You hear me, Bell? No working artillery."

"Aww . . ." Bell groaned, but he was smiling, too.

"So we're basically building a box that doesn't go anywhere?"

"Oh, no, Tam. I want you to correct the design flaw. That's part of the challenge!"

"But . . ."

But Mr. Randolph had already strolled away from their table, leaving the three boys on their dinosaurs, still marveling at da Vinci's drawing. Tam scooted the paper forward.

"So what are we going to use to make this? Cardboard? Foam board?"

Timmy asked, "Did they have cardboard in Renaissance Italy?"

"Well, we can't Google it. Maybe if we find some sticks outside, we can—"

"My garage," Bell interjected.

"Huh?"

"We're going to build it in my garage," he repeated, his grin growing wider by the second. As the idea formed, as his mind made its measurements, they pushed everything else away: his homework, Daelynn's disruptions, even Parker Hellickson.

Bell had something to build . . .

"You're not seriously thinking that we're going to make this . . ."

". . . life-size!" Timmy finished, his smile matching Bell's.

"But the thing must be, like, twelve feet in diameter!"

"Fifteen," Bell said reverently. "And seven feet high."

"Without power tools?" Tam shook his head. "And where are we going to get all that wood? The nails? The—"

"Leave that up to me," Bell said, rubbing his hands together. "You guys just clear your schedules for the weekends."

"No problem," Timmy replied proudly. "I already told Ma and Dad that I'd be working on the Creator Contest between now and May. 'Anything to keep you off the computer!' Dad said. He's gonna love this."

"I have soccer practice every weekend," Tam said.

"Come over after!"

"I have oboe lessons, too."

"After that?"

"Swim practice."

Timmy snorted. "You do know why it's called Saturday, right? By the end of it, you're supposed to have *sat ur* butt down all day."

Tam rolled his eyes. "We literally just learned this in social studies. Saturn was the Roman god of—"

"Yeah, my story is better."

Bell laughed. "We can work on it in the evenings, after dinner."

"You do eat dinner, right?" Timmy asked.

"Fine. I can come over on Saturdays after dinner, *if* my parents say it's okay."

"Challenge accepted, then?" Bell said, and he held up his hand, fingers extended like the spikes of a styracosaurus's crest.

Sighing, Tam made a fist and rammed it into Bell's hand, the clubbed tail of an ankylosaur. "Challenge accepted."

Timmy mashed both of his hands against the locked-together fist and palm, curling his fingers and then wiggling them rapidly while he growled and yipped, the velociraptors tearing apart their prey. Gleefully, he said, "Challenge accepted!"

"That looked like fun! Did you guys just make that up, or do you always do it?"

All three boys turned to face Daelynn, who had snuck over from her team's table and was peering over Bell's shoulder at the sketch of the tank.

"Hey, no fair cheating!" Timmy snapped, and he dove to cover the paper with his arms.

"How is she going to cheat? Her team has an entirely different invention, genius."

As Timmy swatted at Tam, Bell rubbed the back of his neck.

"It's just a thing we've always done."

"I wonder if—"

Bell cleared his throat. "Um, you should get back to your team."

Daelynn peeked at Rachel and Chris. They were shoulder to shoulder over their da Vinci plans, whispering and pointing.

"They're . . . well . . . kind of busy right now. They said they'd let me know what I can do once they're ready, since they already have a system in place."

So do I, thought Bell. *Lots of them.*

"Anyway," she continued. "I think your design looks neat. Like a house on wheels!"

Bell shrugged.

And then the room went dark.

"Mr. Randolph?" Rachel asked.

From the front of the room, they heard his rumbling voice. "You have thirty minutes to start work on your projects. You'll need to delegate responsibilities, come up with a materials list, and begin your designs. In the bins below your tables you'll find pencils, rulers, scrap paper, and candles."

A flame flared to life from Mr. Randolph's desk. Delicately pinched between his thumb and forefinger was a safety match, the fire flickering as he lowered it to a white-wicked candle. With his shadow cast behind him on the wall like that of a giant, their favorite teacher raised his hands, squared his shoulders, and took a bow.

"Ladies and gentlemen," Mr. Randolph declared, "the Creator Contest has begun!"

When he could see again, Bell looked around for Daelynn, but she was already back with her team, her chin in her palm as she watched Chris and Rachel strategize.

Da Vinci's tank, eh?

> Yeah! Only we have to fix the design flaw.

The gear thing, if memory serves.

> Right.

Are you excited to build it?

> Super excited. Especially because I actually know what I'm doing, unlike in a certain puzzle . . .

I told you I'd answer all your questions.

> Great. How's about this: Are the objects made out of wood?

Do you want them to be made out of wood?

> Um . . . yeah? They'd float then.

Okay! Then they're made out of wood.

> Does the shepherd have any tools to build with?

Do you want her to have tools to build with?

> Dad . . . Is there even an answer to this puzzle?

Yeah. You want it?

> No! I'm not giving up. Just strange that it doesn't matter if the stuff is wood or if she has tools.

Who said it didn't matter?

> You! Just now!

No. I said you could pick whether any of those things are true or not.

> If I can pick, won't my answer make your answer wrong?

72

😊 I hope it does! That's my favorite dream: that one day my son will out-design me. A good engineer knows there's more than one way to build something. A great engineer understands that there's always a *better* way to build something, waiting to be discovered. Heck, if there wasn't, we'd all be out of a job . . .

🔔 But there is an answer . . .

😊 Yes, Bell. There's an answer. I'm just not going to be disappointed if you discover a better one.

🔔 I get it.

😊 So what solutions have you tried so far?

🔔 Lots. I lined them up in order, but they don't reach all the way across, and I tried building an arch out of them, but they don't quite connect, and I thought about leaving gaps, but I wasn't sure if the sheep could jump across them.

😊 Whoa. That list is a lot to digest. You might want to use a colon.

🔔 What?

😊 :

🔔 Why?

😊 A LOT TO DIGEST.

🔔 ?

😊 A COLON, BELL.

🔔 I rarely understand what you're talking about.

😊 JUST *PUNCTUATING* OUR CONVERSATION WITH A LITTLE HUMOR.

🔔 Ugh. Good night, Dad. Love you.

😊 Love you, Bell.

CHAPTER TEN

On Fridays, Village Green Elementary served Cincinnati-style chili: spaghetti, complete with all the fixings—beans, onions, cheese, and even the little oyster crackers. It was one of the most popular lunches, and kids lined up down the hallway to get it. Often, it'd take fifteen minutes just to make it through the line . . . which was perfect, because Parker always bought his lunch.

By design, Bell always packed his, which, even calculating conservatively, gave him ten minutes to check in with Tam about the weekend trip to the scrapyard. He plunked his lunch box down next to Tam's and slid in.

"So, did you talk to your mom and dad?" Bell asked.

Tam held up a finger. His mouth was full of tuna fish sandwich.

"Yeah," he finally replied. "I can make it. My mom doesn't want us spending money, though. She says the fee for Creator Club is high enough already."

Bell grinned. "My mom has us covered. The guys at the

scrapyard are good friends of hers; we can probably get stuff for free."

"Fine," Tam said, and he took another bite of tuna.

Bell set his notebook down on the table and flipped to page 102. Surrounded by drawings of cannons firing cookies across the page was the list of supplies Bell had drafted that morning.

"What do you think of this stuff, to start?" Bell asked, but Tam wasn't looking. He had stopped chewing, too. Instead, he was staring straight ahead . . .

. . . right at Daelynn, who had sat across from them. Her special must have let out early, because in front of her was a Styrofoam tray full of spaghetti, covered in cinnamony sauce, beans, chopped-up onions, and a melty mountain of cheese. She was poking at the impressive mound gently with a plastic fork, and she looked skeptical.

"Is . . . is this why you packed your lunches today?" she asked.

Bell shook his head, and he dragged his notebook closer.

Mistake.

"Wow!" Daelynn gasped. "Cool drawings! Can I see?" She slid her chili to the side and reached for the notebook. Bell snatched it up before she could grab it, though.

"Geez . . . sorry . . . ," she murmured.

"It's okay," Bell said. "I just—"

"Bell's notebook is like his life," Tam said. Bell glared at him. "What? Am I lying?"

Daelynn nodded. "Oh, don't worry. I totally get it. You should see my sketchbook! If someone tried to tug it toward this goopy pile of . . ."

"Deliciousness," Tam supplied.

"Drippiness," Daelynn countered. "I'd freak out, too. You want to see?"

Bell looked down at his watch nervously. When he raised his head, though, she was already pulling that heavy, bound sketchbook out of her backpack. She slid the chili well out of the way, wiped her sleeve across the table just to be sure, and propped her book up like a science fair display board.

Then, she turned to the first page.

"Whoa . . . ," Tam whispered.

"Holy . . . ," Bell began.

"I work on them every day," Daelynn said proudly.

She'd have to, Bell thought.

Her drawings were stunning.

A meadow, surrounded by trees, teemed with wildflowers of every hue. Moths and butterflies crawled around the margins, so detailed that Bell could see the individual feathers of each antennae. At the center of the meadow were two horses, drawn as lifelike as Bell had ever seen. And yet despite the accuracy, there was something utterly magical, a sense that it couldn't be real, simply because reality was never quite that vivid.

"They keep going," Daelynn declared, and she turned

the page. Amazingly, the picture seemed to continue, that same meadow rolling along, unbroken even by the razor's edge of the paper. It was so very much like Bell's own designs, except that where his were precise, Daelynn's seemed to grow organically, even chaotically, like she had planted a seed on page one and had been nurturing it to bloom ever since. A stream trickled through page two, and a majestic mountain range rose in the background. And everywhere, everywhere, horses grazed and galloped through the scene.

It was, in Bell's estimation, a masterpiece. *Is this what kids do in homeschool all day?* he wondered, and he let himself get a little lost in the beauty of it. At least, until . . .

"What're those?" Parker spat as he dropped his plateful of chili down next to Tam's lunch. Daelynn had to yank her sketchbook back quickly to avoid the spatter. Bell's whole body tensed. His appetite seemed to sprint out the door; he wished he could have followed it.

"My drawings," Daelynn replied matter-of-factly.

Bell went pale.

"Are those cows or something?" Parker quipped, and he nudged Tam, who shrugged.

"They're horses," Daelynn said proudly, pointing with a plum-painted fingernail. "This one is a palomino Andalusian. These are Missouri Fox Trotters, and over here is a leopard Knabstrupper."

Parker snorted. "Was that supposed to be, like, in English?"

Daelynn smiled, baring her braces.

"That *was* English," she said cheerfully, using the exact same tone Bell's old kindergarten teacher did when reciting the ABCs. "Here. I'll help. *Miss-our-i*: a state. *Fox*: a type of fuzzy animal with red fur. *Trot-ter*: something that trots. See? English!"

Parker's eyes went wide, and the corner of his mouth started twitching.

Tam swallowed audibly.

Bell nearly fell out of his chair. He wanted to hide before Parker exploded, but he didn't dare draw attention to himself. Not when all of it was so squarely on Daelynn.

After a few more tense, silent moments, she shrugged, then swept her sketchbook into her backpack. Picking up her chili with her other hand, Daelynn said, "Oh . . . there's Ashi. I'll—"

She never got to finish her sentence. With a sickening Styrofoam squeal, her tray cracked in two. Everyone knew the trays were flimsy—they were two-hands mandatory. But someone new to a public school cafeteria? Someone new to school entirely?

She didn't know.

Bell watched in horror as a landslide of steaming chili cascaded from the tray. Like a spaghetti-limbed octopus, the liquidy mass slithered its way across the table . . .

. . . then down . . .

. . . and into Parker's lap.

"Oh my gosh!" Daelynn gasped. "I am so sorry! I have napkins!"

It looked for a moment like she might come around the table to help Parker, but he shot her such a hideous look—all bared teeth and eyeballs and bottomless nostrils—that she froze. Two teachers swept in quickly, one cleaning the table while the other tried to navigate Parker to the trash can without dumping more melted cheese on the floor. When he sat back down, there was a big, greasy stain down his shirt and pants, and he was fuming.

For the rest of lunch, Bell hung his head. Though Tam was between them, he could hear every word Parker said about Daelynn. Most of it was terrible and offensive, with words that would've gotten Bell grounded for good at home. Tam seemed to ignore most of it, but every so often, he'd nod. Parker seized on it, like he was throwing his spaghetti noodles at the wall to see what stuck. Worse, some of it *was* clever, and Bell found himself stifling a smile several times.

It was enough that, by the end of lunch, Bell felt nauseous. At least, when the bell rang, Parker was still so obsessed with Daelynn that he ignored Bell completely. And at recess, Bell didn't have to wait by the doors until Parker was gone. He cleared out right away, storming to his locker to get a change of clothes. Bell was able to just walk outside, and he got a good spot in the four-square lines.

"Bell, man! You're gonna get to play today!" Timmy said, grinning from his king spot in the number one square.

"I guess so," Bell replied. Sure enough, he got in within seconds . . .

. . . and was out on the very first serve, which is what happens to someone who normally has to hide for the entire recess.

CHAPTER ELEVEN

"What do you mean you can only come for an hour?" Timmy shouted into the phone. Bell flinched; he was the one actually holding the phone. Timmy was standing next to him. It was Tam they had called.

Tam's voice, on speakerphone, came through all staticky. "Something else came up."

"But this is for school," Timmy protested.

"And we've been talking about going to the scrapyard all week!" Bell added.

"This other thing is for school, too."

Bell looked at Timmy, who shrugged.

"What else could there be? We don't have any projects due next week."

There was a long pause.

"Tam?"

"It's Parker, okay? His dad told him we could start working on our float for the Spring Festival."

Bell scowled.

"You were with us first, Tam," Timmy whined.

"Actually, I wasn't. I helped Parker with his float in fourth grade, too."

Timmy scuffed at the carpet in Bell's living room with his foot. "The parade is stupid, anyway. It's the same every year: a bunch of random Cub Scout troops and book clubs and gymnastics squads taping posters to wagons and dragging them down the street. I've watched the Rose Bowl Parade. *Those* are floats. Not whatever Parker, Justin, and Shipman are going to slap together. What about the hammers? The drills? The chainsaws?"

"Chainsaws?" Bell asked. "For a float?"

"If I were building it, there'd be chainsaws," Timmy declared, and he buzzed his lips together, spitting everywhere while he pretended to cut Bell's couch in two.

"Gee," Tam said, "I wonder why you guys weren't invited to join a group."

"People should invite Bell. He'd design the best float ever!" Timmy said once his impression ran out of gas.

Bell shook his head. "That's okay. I'm not exactly falling over myself to get invitations to Parker's house. I'd much rather go to the scrapyard, but I don't think we're going to have enough time now. Only an hour?"

"You guys should go without me," Tam offered.

"We're supposed to do all this together."

They heard Tam sigh. "I promise I'll write a good progress report. Why wouldn't I? If you get all the materials, it's actually helping me."

Bell's shoulders slumped, but Timmy jumped in. "It's cool, then. We'll scope out the supplies for the tank. You satisfy your parents."

"Thanks," Tam said. "This means I'll have time to eat dinner."

And then he hung up.

Bell and Timmy got their winter hats and coats on, and it was just as Bell was wriggling his fingers into his gloves that his mom came downstairs. Together, they loaded up the back of Mrs. Kirby's truck with the pile of pipes, plywood, and metal sheeting that had accumulated in their garage. She explained that lots of the piping was copper, which the guys at the scrapyard loved.

Once the truck was loaded, and Bell and Timmy had buckled in, they set off. On the way, Mrs. Kirby filled them in.

"Good news, guys. We'll be able to use nails, crank drills, planes, chisels, most of our saws, and any of the other hand tools I've got in the cabinet. I also called Mr. Randolph and asked him if I could do some welding, since we don't exactly have a blacksmith's forge in our basement. He said it was okay, provided you're there to watch and learn."

"He didn't have a problem with us trying to build da Vinci's tank life-size in the garage?"

Mrs. Kirby laughed. "On the contrary, it sounds like he expected it. Your reputation precedes you, Joseph Bell Kirby."

Timmy always laughed when Mrs. Kirby used Bell's full name. They had chosen it to honor Joseph Bell, the head engineer for the *RMS Titanic* who sacrificed himself to keep the lights on while the lifeboats were loaded. Even so, it made Bell grumpy. His frown didn't last long, though, because they pulled up to the scrapyard a few minutes later.

As Reggie and Mac Buckman, the owners of Buckman's Haul-'n'-Scrap, came out to hug Mrs. Kirby and offer her coffee, Bell and Timmy slipped out of their side of the truck, boots splashing down in the mud to the side of the gravel driveway. Timmy went to beg to open the gate, and when Reggie gave him the go-ahead, he scrambled into the little guard shed to press the button. As the gate beeped and slowly started pulling open, Bell took in the sights, letting his mind wander.

A pile of car doors, blue and silver and red and black, sat just inside the fence, and Bell's mind created the cars around them. That white one came from a little hatchback. The greenish rusty one was from an old pickup truck, perhaps. And the one with the single racing stripe down the side used to call a Porsche home. As good as Bell's brain was at deconstructing things, it was even more adept at putting them together, and he liked nothing better than a pile of old parts to build with. It was Timmy who saw the stories behind stuff. Bell was into the *potential*.

When the gate was open, Timmy ran ahead, Bell slogging through the mud to catch up. His friend zeroed in on the striped door immediately. "Wow! I bet this, like, flew off in the middle of a race! Driver is going a hundred and sixty, easy, and then he gets clipped into the wall. *Krickathoom!* His door goes flying off. Nearly decapitates someone in the crowd, but dude keeps driving, right? And then at the very end, his car spins out, but he jumps away, 'cause he's got no door, right? And the momentum of his car throws him across the finish line first. Guy walks up to the podium, grabs the trophy, and pours milk on his head like he doesn't even care."

Bell stared at his best friend. "Milk on his head?"

"Yeah. It's a thing they do. Look it up."

"Sure," Bell said.

The rest of the scrapyard was just as fascinating; they both could have stayed all night under the big floodlights, rooting through the mounds of metal and spare parts, picking up pieces and wondering what each could have been or might still be. But when Bell's mom backed the truck up through the gate, she put them to work immediately. Bell held open his notebook like a shopping list, rattling off parts and pieces they might need, while Mrs. Kirby, Reggie, and Mac loaded the stuff in the truck. Timmy examined each piece carefully once it was in the flatbed. "Quality control," he called himself. By the time they were done, Timmy had to evacuate; there wasn't enough room for him.

"Think you got it all?" Reggie asked, taking off his ball cap and wiping a sleeve across his forehead. It was cold, but he had still worked up a sweat.

"Bell?" Mrs. Kirby said.

"We should be good!" he declared.

Mac closed up the back of the truck and slapped his mittened hands down on the tailgate.

"You sure about this, Major? What you've got in here ain't worth a quarter of the copper you brought."

Mrs. Kirby smiled. "Consider the extra as payment for all the times you've let the boys have the run of the place."

"You kidding? We have more fun when they're here!" Reggie said, and he popped open the passenger-side door for the kids to clamber in.

On the way home, Bell flipped through his notebook while Timmy squirmed around in his seat to watch over all the da Vinci–approved salvage they had scored, making sure they didn't lose any of it going over bumps. Eventually, his wriggling brought him in line with Bell.

"Hey, what did you draw there?" Timmy asked, sticking his head right in Bell's way. Bell jerked his notebook to the side.

"Nothing."

"Were those parts for the tank? Because I don't remember a faucet in da Vinci's design. Could be cool, though: a frosty mug of root beer on tap while you're rollin' into battle."

"Not for the tank," Bell sighed. "It's a puzzle my dad gave me."

"Lemme see!" Timmy chirped, and he grabbed at the

notebook. When Bell yanked it away again, Timmy pursed his lips. Then his eyes got big, and he grinned.

"Don't you dare, Timmy," Bell whispered.

"I wanna see! Please, Bell! Please?" Timmy whined, much louder this time.

"Bell, let your friend see your notebook," Mrs. Kirby muttered without taking her eyes off the road.

"Fine," Bell said, and he flipped to the page where he had drawn the puzzle originally. Timmy looked at it for thirty seconds, then handed it back.

"Easy, dude. Just put all that strange stuff in the water and let her climb across."

"They don't fit. I've tried measuring and everything."

"Let 'em float there, then, and the sheepies can jump across. If they can handle jumping fences, they can handle that."

"It's a river, dude," Bell huffed. "If the pieces floated, they'd be washed away."

"Fine. So you take that long bow tie–looking piece and put it on top of the one that looks like an arrowhead."

"I think it's a spinning top."

"Whatever. Put it on top of that, like balanced and everything. Then you use it like a catapult. She can test the distance by chucking those other little pieces over—you know, just so none of the sheep splat against the far side, or get impaled on the sign, or get eaten by the piranhas."

"There aren't any piranhas!"

"Oh, there's totally piranhas, man. That's piranha city, for sure."

Bell face-palmed. "It doesn't matter. A catapult isn't a bridge. And even if you could catapult the sheep across—which is ridiculous anyway—she'd still be stuck on the opposite bank in the end."

"Yep. Secure in the knowledge that her sheep were safe. We can't have everything in life, you know."

Bell laughed, and they spent the remainder of the drive home brainstorming more wild solutions to the puzzle.

As they pulled up to Timmy's house to drop him off, Mrs. Kirby said, "Too bad Tam couldn't make it."

"Yeah, but he had to go work on a Spring Festival float."

Mrs. Kirby drummed her fingers on the steering wheel.

"I seem to recall that anyone can make one. Why don't you guys ever give it a shot?"

"We have Creator Club to worry about," Bell muttered.

"And Tam's working over at Parker's," Timmy added. Bell cringed.

"Ah," Mrs. Kirby replied.

Once Timmy was safely inside and they were on the road again, Bell's mom said, "Bet you'd design an awesome float, though."

Bell flipped his notebook open, taking one more look at his dad's puzzle.

She was right.

He probably would.

Are there piranhas in the water?

Do you want there to be piranhas in the water?

No. Timmy thought there might be, though.

I didn't mean to. He just kind of saw. That's not cheating, is it?

Ahhh, you asked Timmy for help?

Heck no! I'm glad you asked for help. Excellent engineers always do.

His ideas were, um . . .

You can say that again.

Different than yours?

Different than yours?

Dad . . .

I know Timmy. I can imagine what sorts of ideas he had. Let me guess . . . not all the sheep survive his version . . .

Those piranhas? They'd be well-fed by the time Timmy was through.

Still, talking to him could help. You might just need a different perspective on this one. I deviously designed it to be difficult for you, Bell.

So, what? It's easy for someone else?

Maybe? Probably? That's the beauty of people, Bell. I can assemble a model of a 1988 Lamborghini Countach in under six minutes, but I can't play a trumpet to save my life. I tried once. Ever heard a walrus belch, Bell?

Uh, no?

Neither have I, but I'm betting my trumpet playing was a spot-on imitation.

Nasty.

Speaking of which, I booked my next gig. My trumpet and I are headlining your senior prom.

That's not for another seven years, Dad.

Tick tock, Bell.

Dad!

I love you, Bell.

I love you too.

CHAPTER TWELVE

B ell knew something was off as soon as he got to school on Monday. Parker always held court in the hallway until the last possible minute, forcing Bell to lug his heavy backpack into the classroom without dropping off his books first. But this morning, almost as soon as Bell had spotted Parker, he had ducked into the classroom, dragging Justin and Tam with him. It put Bell on high alert.

Holding his backpack tight and his notebook tighter, Bell crept toward his locker, eyes on Mrs. Vicker's door. Had Parker grown wise to Bell's system? Was he waiting just inside the classroom, ready to spring out and scare Bell as soon as he got close? Was there some disgusting leftover milk carton trap set in his locker, ready to dump curdled grossness all over his shirt as soon as he opened it? The teacher on hall duty moseyed into view, which made Bell feel safer. He decided to risk it.

Currie Oaks and Adrienne Monet were sitting just in

front of Bell's locker, and they were as surprised to see him as he was to be there. They scooted to either side to let him in. He grimaced. With an audience watching, he couldn't go through all his protocols: sniff his locker, wipe the handle with a tissue, and take everything out of his backpack first so that he could maintain sight lines down the hallway for as long as possible before his open locker door blocked his view. Of course, he also couldn't back down.

Bell took a deep breath, reached out, and tugged open his locker.

Instinctively, he flinched.

Nothing happened.

He looked around. Currie and Adrienne were chatting around his legs, almost like he wasn't even there. The teacher had stopped to admire another kid's sneakers. A dozen fourth graders milled by, bumping into lockers, the walls, and one another like bouncing off stuff was the only way they knew how to move.

With a sigh of relief, Bell put his books into his locker, grabbed his pencil box, and closed the door. The lines along his shoulders where his heavy backpack had bitten felt better already, and he imagined what it would be like to have Mrs. Vicker smile at him when he came in, rather than frowning at how stooped over with book weight he was.

Inside the classroom, all seemed normal, too. Mrs. Vicker was arranging the schedule magnets on the board, and most of the kids were hunched over their morning work. Bell usually had to go all the way around the classroom to get to his desk, because Parker sat closer to the door than he did. This time, though, Parker was at Justin's desk, near the back corner. Bell was able to walk straight down the aisle to his seat.

From his desk, Bell could hear Parker speaking, though he couldn't make out the words. A familiar prickle crawled up his neck—he knew what usually happened after Parker was done plotting. But when he snuck a glance back, Parker and Justin weren't looking at him. In fact, he might as well have been invisible. He followed the path of their eyes to the front of the classroom.

Right to Daelynn.

She had obviously finished her morning work, because she had her sketchbook out. She was wearing a blue puffy skirt, almost like a ballerina's tutu, and tights with storm clouds and lightning bolts running up and down the sides, along with her usual red sneakers. Bell noticed that her legs bounced when she was drawing—not nervous-like, but just tapping, like there was a song only she could hear. She was drawing with a yellow colored pencil in her left hand, and in her right she held about fifteen more, shoved point-first between the fingers of her fist, five at a time. They were arranged there by color—blues and greens in one row; reds, yellows, and oranges between her middle and ring fingers, and browns, grays, and black in the back. Bell found himself nodding appreciatively as she finished with the yellow, swapped it for an orange, and kept going.

She had a system.

When Mrs. Vicker was done with the schedule, she snapped her fingers twice. Parker rushed to his seat. He didn't even slow down to whisper something mean in Bell's ear, or to kick the leg of Bell's chair.

Yep. Something was definitely off. But Bell honestly didn't know if that was a bad thing or not.

Their first special of the day was gym, and it was the easiest trip there all year. Parker actually waited in the classroom after Mrs. Vicker dismissed the class, letting Bell slip out first. Since all the fifth graders had gym together, Bell found Timmy almost immediately.

"What're we playing today?" Bell asked.

"Floor hockey," Timmy replied, pointing to the big bin in the corner of the gym. A thicket of plastic handles sprouted out.

"I hate floor hockey," Bell murmured. They had done an entire unit of it in fourth grade, and not a day had gone by when Bell didn't have bruises on his ankles and shins from Parker "accidentally" slapping his legs with his stick.

"Good thing you're here early," Timmy said. "Instead of getting put with some randoms, we can be partners for once. That way I can watch your back."

Bell nodded, and he shot hoops with Timmy until class was about to begin. He kept a lookout the entire time, but Parker didn't show up until right before the gym teachers blew their whistles. Bell ran to his line with Timmy. It wasn't until the gym teachers took attendance that he noticed Daelynn wasn't there.

"Gower? Where's Gower?" Ms. Waxman shouted.

Ashi raised her hand.

"Daelynn's here! Or, she's supposed to be. I just mean she's in school."

"I'll call the offi—"

"Wait!" Ashi exclaimed, and everyone turned toward the gym doors. Daelynn was hobbling in, one shoe crumpled beneath her foot, only half on.

Bell shook his head.

She had been flat-tired.

Ms. Waxman jogged over to Daelynn, smiling and sweeping her hand toward the rest of the kids as if to welcome her. However, when she got closer, she put both hands on Daelynn's shoulders, leaning forward to speak with her. It was hard to tell if Daelynn was crying, but her body trembled like she was. And when she pointed at Parker, all fifty-four pairs of eyes snapped on him. He looked around, then held out his hands and mouthed, "What? Me?"

Ms. Waxman led Daelynn to her office at the rear of the gym, and then she collected Parker. Bell could hear him protesting the entire way. The assistant gym teacher, Mr. Long, led the class from there. Without Parker to pick on him, Bell had a blast. He even scored a goal.

Still, he wasn't so absorbed that he didn't sneak a look through the plexiglass windows into Ms. Waxman's office from time to time. In doing so, he was able to see Daelynn, her arms crossed, and Parker, his hands moving every which way as he explained something. It wasn't until midway through the game that they emerged, Daelynn frowning, Parker shrugging, and Ms. Waxman rolling her eyes. Bell looked away as they marched past him and joined their teams. And though he had his best gym class all year, he couldn't help but feel sorry for Ms. Waxman; floor hockey was one of her favorites, and she had missed the first half of the game.

He felt a little bad that Daelynn had missed it, too.

He felt even worse because he was pretty sure he knew what had happened.

But mostly, he just felt glad it hadn't happened to him.

CHAPTER THIRTEEN

The next three weeks flew by. Bell spent every weekend in the garage with his friends, working on the tank. It was coming along, too: Bell, Timmy, and Tam had managed to cut all the scrap lumber down to perfect, even pieces. Tam was a pro with the saw, and Timmy loved using the plane to scrape off long, curly slivers of wood, which he collected and stapled together to form a pretty righteous beard.

On weeknights, Bell put on the heavy gloves, goggles, and safety apron to help his mom in the corner of the garage they had named "the Smithy." According to what they found in the library, blowtorches had been around in some form or other long enough to count, so he got to use Sir Weldmore to cut and fuse the metal cranks that would make the tank move. By the end of that third week, they had most of the parts ready for assembly.

School was going every bit as well . . . sort of. Bell kept to his systems, following the schedules and routes that made him feel comfortable and safe. But he noticed that the hot spots—places where Parker tended to trap Bell if he wasn't careful—weren't so dangerous anymore. He was able to get to his locker more often. He made it to classes on time. And he never realized how big a luxury it was to be able to go to the bathroom between math and their computer special.

It wasn't that Parker was gone. He was there every day. But it seemed to Bell as though he had developed a sort of invisible shield. Parker's attention just slipped off him, like a tiger that decided it no longer had a taste for rabbit. They even faced off against each other in floor hockey. Bell had closed his eyes before the puck dropped, but when he opened them, Parker had already shot past him—no slaps to the shins or shoulder shoves to speak of.

In fact, in the last gym class, Parker even passed to Bell for a goal. It was the happiest he'd felt in gym all year.

It lasted all of ten minutes.

Ms. Waxman asked for volunteers to help put the equipment away, and for the first time since third grade, Bell raised his hand. The teacher had to blink a couple of times to make sure it was really Bell Kirby agreeing to do anything but rush out of the gym as fast as he could. Once she was satisfied, though, she called on him immediately. Bell actually had fun sorting the sticks by size and putting them away. Ms. Waxman even called him one of her best helpers. That's why, as he slipped into the hallway, he was holding his head high for a change.

As a result, he saw Daelynn, leaning forward over the terrible drinking fountain. Her glasses were in her left hand while her right mashed the button as hard as she could. Even though she was on her tiptoes, putting her entire weight into it, she still only managed to get a bubble or two. Bell thought about guiding her to the better fountain, but just as he stepped forward, Parker burst out of the boys' bathroom. Bell gasped, and by habit, he ducked around the corner to hide.

Not before seeing Parker smash into Daelynn on his way past, though.

Bell felt his heart thudding in his chest. He put his hand on the wall and peeked around the corner. Daelynn was holding one hand over her mouth while the other swept around on the ground, trying to find her glasses. They were right there next to her knee, but the tears in her eyes were probably making it twice as hard to see. Bell could have just walked up and handed them to her.

Instead, he ran the other way, taking his back route to Mrs. Vicker's class. When he arrived, Parker was already at his desk, scribbling on a math test Mrs. Vicker had returned while they were at gym. Daelynn was nowhere to be seen.

Not even after class began.

Or five minutes after that. Or ten.

It was a long twenty minutes later that Mr. Hellickson popped his head in.

"Sorry to bother you all!" he said cheerfully. "Mrs. Vicker, I'm returning one of your wayward lambs."

He stood to the side, and Daelynn shuffled in behind him. She had her glasses on, but Bell could see the tears behind them all the same. Before she could get to her seat, Mr. Hellickson grabbed her by the shoulders from behind and held her there, like he was presenting some kind of robot he'd invented.

"Seems this student of yours, Mrs. Vicker . . ."

"Daelynn," Bell whispered.

"Seems she got bumped in the hallway. Unfortunately, she didn't have her glasses on, and she was getting a drink at the time, so she didn't see who did it. I said I'd make her feel better by asking if anyone saw what happened."

The entire classroom erupted in high-pitched chair scoots as twenty-three kids all started twisting at the same time, craning to see if anyone raised their hand or stood up. Parker was the twistiest and craniest of them all, and his eyes roved over the room like a prison spotlight searching for escapees. Bell sank down in his seat. A strange, metallic taste filled his mouth, like he was going to be sick.

He swallowed nervously.

He ran his tongue rapidly beneath his chipped tooth.

But Bell didn't say a word.

At least, not until lunchtime, when he told Timmy about the lumpy feeling growing in his gut.

"I get it, Bell. It's like you ate a magic bean."

"Um, it's not that type of stomach pain . . ."

Timmy shook his head. "I'm not talking taco trouble, man. Pretend a wizard gives you this magic bean, right? And he says if you eat it, your troubles will disappear. So you're all like, 'Seriously? Gimme that bean!'"

Bell arched an eyebrow.

"But right as you're about to eat it, the wizard yells, 'Halt! Forsooth!'—'cause, you know, they're always saying stuff like *forsooth*—'Whomsoever eats the Bean of the Spleen—'"

"Bean of the Spleen?"

"That's what I said. Or what he said. Anyway, 'Bean of the Spleen shall experience yon happiness and stuff, forsooth and hearken! But be forewarned, ye olde Bean of the Spleen shall sprout in thy belly, and grow there until yon belly explodes, forsooth forsooth!' And then a beanstalk grows out of your stomach and leads to a golden goose, or something. But you don't get the goose, 'cause you're dead."

"On account of the exploding belly?"

Timmy nodded gravely. "Bean of the Spleen, man. Gets you every time."

Bell nodded, too, and he cast a glance at Daelynn. She sat at the end of the table. Ashi and Adrienne were next to her, but they weren't talking. Daelynn wasn't eating much, either.

It was probably hard for her, what with her swollen lip.

Bell noticed other things, too, as the weeks went by. Daelynn was absent a lot, and she even missed Valentine's

Day, though Mrs. Vicker made a box for her cards anyway. When she got back, she read through them during morning work and suddenly jumped out of her seat to run into the hall. Mrs. Vicker rushed after her.

Bell didn't need to hear Parker laughing to know whose valentine had made Daelynn upset. He also knew from experience that the card was likely typed, with no way of tracing it back to its author. After all, his mom had spent an hour in Mr. Hellickson's office last year at the same time, waving around a letter just like it.

So yes, he knew exactly what was going on, but he also had years of experience with what Parker would do to him if he interfered. So Bell focused on school, the tank, and his dad's puzzle, using his system to avoid Daelynn as much as possible. It worked, too; the only time he talked to her was when Mrs. Vicker paired them up to work on a vocabulary sheet together. Even then, Bell had spent the first three minutes staring at the paper silently. When he finally peeked at Daelynn, she wasn't paying attention. Her arms were crossed, and she chewed her pencil eraser nervously. Every so often, her eyes would flick toward the right side of the room.

Bell didn't need to look to guess who she was worried about.

"Um . . . ," he finally mumbled. She twitched, startled, like she had forgotten he was there. Then she bent over her worksheet.

"Sorry . . . I'm sorry . . . ," she said softly.

"It's okay. We still have plenty of time," Bell replied.

"Oh," she said, and she started doodling in the corner of her worksheet—nothing fancy, just a fence-like pattern. Another minute of silence passed.

Bell scratched his head. He looked at his watch. And then he said, "So, uh . . . got any pets?"

That got a little smile, at least. It disappeared quickly, though, and Daelynn slumped lower in her chair. After a few moments, she said, "We used to, back in Oregon. Four gorgeous horses. I'd go visit them at the stables every day with my friends."

"You had *friends*?" Bell asked. The words tasted like dirt as soon as he said them.

Daelynn's lip started to quiver.

"I'm . . . I didn't mean it like that. I just figured . . . you know . . . because of homeschool . . ."

She slowly shook her head. "What exactly do you think homeschool is, Bell?"

Bell blushed furiously. "I . . . I actually have no clue."

"It was hard work," she said, pointing down at their worksheet. "Harder than this. But it was nice, too. We . . . my dad and I . . . we could set our own schedule. Work in the morning, go see the horses in the afternoon."

"What happened to them?"

"We had to sell them so we could move here."

Bell shifted in his seat. "Aren't there any stables around here you could have—"

She sniffled and put her pencil down.

"It wasn't that," she said. "My mom's company went broke, and when she got a new job in Cincinnati . . . well, we had to leave home. Now my dad has to work, too, so I'm here."

Bell nodded. "Yeah," he replied, and he turned his attention back to his sheet. They finished the exercise in silence, and he hadn't said a word to her since—not even in Creator Club. It was all he could do to push down the guilty feeling in his gut, hoping it wouldn't explode, Bean of the Spleen style. He was almost successful, too.

But then the Woodja hit his desk, and everything blew up.

CHAPTER FOURTEEN

Of all the weapons in Parker's arsenal, Bell feared the Woodja most. It was worse than flat tires and fat lips. Worse than hurtful hallway comments and hateful Valentine's Day cards. Worse even than digs at his mom or weeks of shin bruises.

Most kids viewed the Woodja as an inconvenience. Some even thought of it as a game. In Parker's hands, though, it was a tool. A crowbar to drive between people and pry them apart.

All that from a simple scrap of paper.

All that from a few little words.

Bell suspected something when, in the middle of their Wednesday social studies quiz, Parker got up to sharpen his pencil. Nobody else even bothered to look up from their paper. Then again, nobody else knew Parker's habits like Bell did.

And Bell knew that Parker always used mechanical pencils on his tests.

Bell scrunched up his face as he watched Parker. There were two mechanical pencils by his paper, just sitting there, and his little container of replacement lead was inside his desk. Parker did have something in his hand, but it was a white colored pencil. Bell frowned when Parker sharpened it anyway, even though everyone knew colored pencils could jam up the electric sharpener. Bell, of course, wasn't going to say anything, and Mrs. Vicker didn't look up from her grading, even when Parker slipped the pencil free, peered at the point, and jabbed himself in the thumb with it lightly to make sure it was sharp.

As Parker wandered back to his seat, taking a strange, long route around the desks, Bell stiffened. Daelynn was intent on her quiz, one hand running through her spiky rainbow of hair, the other filling in blanks. Parker slowed down as he neared her seat, the pencil held in his fist like a knife. Bell swallowed, sinking down, and he winced as Parker lifted his hand.

And walked right by her.

Straight toward Bell's desk.

With a sly grin, Parker switched the pencil to his other hand. He reached into his pocket, pulling out a folded piece of lined paper. Casually, as though he had practiced the move a thousand times, Parker let the paper go just as he strode past. It landed silently in Bell's lap, making him flinch.

At first, Bell left it there. But when Parker got back to his seat, he stared at Bell, grinning. It made the hairs on the back of Bell's neck stand up. He tried to concentrate on his quiz, but with Parker leering like a hungry bear, he found it impossible. So he slid the folded paper into his desk where no one else could see, and he opened it. All it said was:

DAELYNN   Y/N

Bell was never exactly sure what a Woodja was asking. "Woodja . . . would ya . . ." Would he what? Talk to Daelynn? Go out on a date with her? Kiss her? What he did know was that it didn't really matter; Parker would fill in whatever meanness he wanted. And there was no right answer, because the whole thing was a trap. Bell had found that out the hard way.

He had circled Y on the one Parker sent around last year for Alli Timberman, and the guys teased him for two weeks before he convinced them he didn't have a crush on her. Worse, because of the things he had to say to prove that he *didn't* like Alli, one of her friends had slapped him at recess. Lesson learned, or so he thought.

Two months later, Parker's Woodja for Brandi Kipling hit his desk. Bell tried to move it on without circling anything, but it kept getting passed back to him, like the world's worst game of hot potato. Bell didn't want to be the one caught with it by the teacher, so he circled N. Immediately afterward, Parker cornered him in the hall, demanding to know why Bell hated Brandi . . . with her standing right there. Bell was so upset that he told his mom about it that night. His mom called the teacher, and the class received a speech from the school guidance counselor the next week about being kind. The whole time, Parker scowled at him, like it was his fault they were missing gym.

So he couldn't circle Y. He couldn't circle N. And he couldn't ignore it.

The perfect trap.

Minutes ticked away. Bell rolled his pencil in his fingers. He snuck a glance at Mrs. Vicker, who was sipping from her coffee mug, and he looked back at Parker. He was smiling so big his teeth were showing, and he made a little "speed it up" motion with his hands. Still, Bell hesitated. Daelynn was drawing in her sketchbook now, oblivious to Parker's scheme.

But Bell knew she'd find out about it soon enough. Parker always made sure of that.

It was only when Mrs. Vicker announced that the quiz was over and that the class had to go get their jackets for recess that Bell decided what to do. With shaking hands, he wrote his reply on the Woodja, then folded it up tight and crammed it into his desk so Mrs. Vicker wouldn't see it as she collected the quizzes. She did arch an eyebrow when she saw that Bell hadn't answered the last two questions, but Bell must have looked so ill that she decided not to press the issue.

At his locker, Bell pretended to be busy, but Parker

slapped his shoulder anyway. So much for his hope that Parker wouldn't be able to find it in Bell's desk.

"Thanks, Belly. Can't wait to read this and share it with . . ."

Parker paused. He had been unfolding the Woodja as he talked and now scanned Bell's words. Bell backed up against his locker, holding his jacket out in front of him like a shield.

At first, Parker's lips were drawn tight. Then, slowly, they started to spread. Then he snickered. And then he cackled, a high-pitched hyena howl. Bell gasped as Parker lunged forward, wrapping his arm around Bell's shoulders and leading him down the hallway and out to the recess field.

"Bell! I thought you were, like, friends with this girl!"

Bell's stomach knotted. It felt worse than the cramps he got after sprinting in gym.

"I . . . not really."

"Well, obviously. Anyway, we've *got* to show everyone this. The look on her face will be hilarious!" Parker crowed.

Bell could only stumble along, cheeks prickling as Parker picked up a convoy of kids on the way. Still more joined outside as they marched past the basketball hoops.

Past the four-square courts.

Over the soccer field.

And straight up to Daelynn.

CHAPTER FIFTEEN

Daelynn was walking the edge of the field with Ashi, kicking a half-deflated playground ball along as she went.

"Hey, Daelynn!" Parker shouted.

She turned around. The ball came to a stop a few feet away, settling down like a drowsy turtle. Bell noticed that Daelynn's hands clenched into fists at her sides, and her lips got all tight.

"What do you want, Parker?" Ashi sighed. She didn't seem pleased to see him, either.

"Check out what Bell did to this Woodja!" Parker exclaimed, and he unfolded it. Bell felt the press of the kids behind him, crowding in to try to read.

"What is a Woodja?" Daelynn asked.

"It's stupid," Ashi replied. "Don't worry about it, whatever it says."

Ashi tried to pull Daelynn away by the sleeve, but

Daelynn didn't budge. Instead, she stared hard at Bell, who felt himself getting smaller and smaller by the second.

"So it seems like even Bell Kirby wants you gone. Check it out!"

Parker held up the Woodja and slowly spun around, letting everyone see what it said. It read,

should DAELYNN go back to oregon? Ⓨ/N

Bell tried to brush Parker's arm off his shoulder, but Parker pulled him in tighter. Ashi grabbed the Woodja out of Parker's hand and tore it up, right there and then, throwing the pieces back at them.

Back at Bell.

"I can't believe you're such a jerk, Bell Kirby," Ashi huffed, and she grabbed Daelynn's hand, tugging her toward the teachers. Bell shoved his hands in his pockets and looked down, but not before catching a glimpse of Daelynn. She was staring at him fiercely, the tears in her eyes making their colors all the more vivid.

He could only offer her a shrug in explanation.

As the rest of the kids dispersed, laughing and chatting, Parker, Justin, and Tam stayed behind with Bell. He shuddered, trying to blink his own tears back. That heaviness in his stomach felt unbearable, and with Daelynn gone, he knew exactly who Parker would turn on as a target now. Sure enough, Parker spun to face him. He wore a familiar, triumphant smirk. Bell prepared himself for the worst.

It didn't come.

Sure, Parker shoved him, but lighter than usual. Almost playfully. Bell glanced at Tam in confusion. Tam looked away.

"That was really funny, Bell. I didn't know you could be so harsh!" Parker said.

"I wasn't trying to be," Bell murmured.

"Dang . . ." Justin whistled. "That's even more cold-blooded."

Parker nodded, and then he held up a hand. The other boys watched as he sank into thought for a moment. Then he snapped his fingers.

"Yup," he declared. "It's decided."

"What is?" Bell asked fearfully, his eyes darting from Parker's mole up to his eyes, then back.

"I thought you were a complete waste of space, Bell. Not gonna lie. But Tam here has been talking you up a bit, and today proves that maybe he was right. I think we can use you."

"Use me?"

"Yeah. Tam says you're the best kid in the grade at planning stuff and building it. I mean, you've got to be, having a mad scientist as a mom and a nerd dad. Plus, that notebook you carry around. That's, like, designs and plans and crap, right?"

Tam nodded. "Yeah. Those are Bell's systems."

Bell shot him a "gee, thanks" look. Tam glanced down at his fingernails.

"So yeah. You should come over on Sunday to help design our Spring Festival float."

Bell blinked.

"Come over?"

"Yeah, like back when we were little kids."

"I don't think that's such—"

Tam added, "I'll be there, too."

Bell scratched his head, and he scuffed his toe in the brown grass.

"C'mon, Bell," Parker said lightly. "I'll be your best friend . . ."

For all the times he had made Bell feel uncomfortable— the teasing, the rumors Parker started about him, the sneaky pushes and shoves and slaps and punches—none of them quite made Bell feel like he did now. It was like a door had suddenly opened in front of him. On this side he was stuck with Parker the bully. On the other side, there was an opportunity for something different. A truce? An easier way? All he had to do was walk through.

Trouble was, getting there meant stepping all over Daelynn.

Bell almost said no. He almost wriggled out of Parker's grasp.

But then he thought about how angry Parker might get

if he turned him down. Life *had* been much easier with Parker's attention on Daelynn, and if there was one thing Bell feared more than anything, it was being back in Parker's crosshairs. So he looked at Justin, who nodded. He looked at Tam, who shrugged. And he looked at Parker, who grinned.

Sighing softly, Bell asked, "What time on Sunday?"

CHAPTER SIXTEEN

The rest of the day, Bell stuck to his systems as closely as he could. He sat at the opposite end of the lunch table from Parker and Tam, and he avoided looking over. On his way to French class, he counted the steps from the trophy case to the door, reassuring himself that it was still twenty-two paces. And after school, he even implemented one of his emergency countermeasures: he didn't stop at his locker before going to Creator Club. He just brought everything with him.

As soon as he got there, he peeked past the door-frame. Mr. Randolph was at his desk. Timmy was at their bench.

Daelynn was nowhere in sight.

Timmy clicked his tongue when Bell dropped his heavy bag in the corner. "No locker stop? That's contingency plan number twelve, right? Parker being Parker again?"

"He invited me over."

Timmy nodded knowingly. "Yeah, I hate it when he . . . Wait, what?"

"He invited me to come over to work on his Spring Festival float. Is Daelynn here?"

"Man, who cares where she is? You said no to Parker, right? He's clearly going to get you there, then lock you in his basement to feed to his dog or something."

"Tam is going to be there."

Timmy twisted a finger in his ear. "I need the nurse to do that beepy thing to test my hearing, 'cause I know I'm not listening to Bell Kirby explain why he's gonna go over to Parker Hellickson's house."

"He asked nicely."

"And I *know* you didn't use the word *nicely* just now."

"C'mon," Bell urged. "We've got to light our candles before Mr. Randolph Renaissances the room."

Tam arrived just as they were watching the first trickles of wax ooze onto the safety plates.

"Tam!" Timmy exclaimed. "You're gonna protect Bell, right?"

"Protect him?" Tam asked absentmindedly. He was rooting through his soccer bag, looking for something. He had already taken out his cleats, shin guards, an old shirt, and a stick of Axe deodorant.

"Yeah! From Parker! Bell's going on Sunday, so you're his bodyguard."

Tam finally found his folder. It was covered in grass stains, but he didn't seem to care.

"Here's my progress reports and my part of the designs. Sorry I can't make it Saturday night."

"But you'll be there Sunday?" Bell asked hopefully.

"Yeah," Tam sighed. "I'll be there Sunday. You don't need a bodyguard, though. Parker is, like, legit excited that you're going."

"Because his dog is hungry?" Timmy asked.

Tam arched an eyebrow. "Parker doesn't have a dog . . ."

"It's still sketchy," Timmy grumbled.

"He wants Bell's help on our float design. It hasn't been coming together so well, and I told him Bell was the best designer I knew."

Bell smiled.

"Students!" Mr. Randolph said once he'd helped the rest of the tables with their candles. "You have one hour to work before the lights come back on. Don't waste it!"

While the other bench groups scrambled to grab materials, Bell and his friends carefully moved their working model from the shelf to their table. As the real tank came together in Bell's garage, they made a miniature one from Popsicle sticks and cut-up colored pencils here. It wasn't pretty—they had to use wood glue instead of nails, and their wheels were made out of sliced-up corks. Still, it was the best they could do without Mrs. Kirby's know-how and Sir Weldmore's flames.

And today was the day they'd see if it worked.

"So," Bell said as he took the top off their model to

117

expose the gears and wheels, "moving forward should be pretty easy. Backward, too."

Timmy nodded. "Yeah. Just crank the left and right sets of wheels at the same time, and you should roll forward."

"Or backward, if you turn them in the opposite direction."

"Cool! Da Vinci built his tank to go in reverse! Dude was way ahead of his time."

Tam shook his head. "Way ahead? They had horses. I'm pretty sure they can go in reverse."

"But sharks can't," Timmy stated.

"I . . . Huh?" Tam wrinkled his nose. Timmy crossed his arms, and Tam gave up. He sighed, pointing down at a pink colored pencil, broken off until it resembled one of the side cranks. "So if you spin this one faster than that one . . ."

"You turn," Bell said. "Because the wheels on one side are going faster than the others, which will push it one way or the other. And if you spin the left side forward and the right side backward, you should be able to turn really, really fast."

Timmy rubbed his hands together. "Ready to try?"

Tam and Bell nodded.

"I'll get the left!" Timmy said, reaching down and pinching the green colored pencil crank.

"I'll take the right," Tam added.

"And I'll record the result," Bell offered, grabbing his notebook.

"Like surgeons huddled over a patient," Mr. Randolph said as he shuffled up to their table. Bell smiled at him, then nodded at his friends.

They slowly started spinning their shafts.

The little wooden tank crawled forward.

Then Timmy's crank broke, toothpick shards and bits of colored pencil scattering across the table.

"Oh, boys, I'm sorry," Mr. Randolph said, patting Bell's shoulder softly. "I guess it's back to the draw—"

"Did you see that?" Timmy blurted.

"That was so cool!" Bell added. "It worked! It moved, like, a whole inch!"

"Two inches," Tam stated confidently.

They high-fived so hard the candles flickered.

Mr. Randolph chuckled. "Man, I love this class," he said, and he wandered over to the next table.

The rest of Creator Club, Bell interviewed Timmy and Tam about what it had been like: How hard did they have to spin the cranks to get it to move? Could they tell they were making progress? Was it harder to start them spinning, or to keep them going? Did it feel stable as it rolled? By the end, they had a ton of good data to take back to the garage, and Bell couldn't wait to share it with his mom.

In fact, he was so excited that he didn't even think about Daelynn.

At least, not until he was on his way home.

With his head buried in his notebook, he almost didn't

see her. He would have walked right past if she hadn't sniffled. The sound drew his eyes to the right, and he spotted her, seated on the cold ground near the after-school pickup lane, her arms circled around her knees. A prickly heat crawled up his neck and into his face, and he forced himself to take a few more steps. Maybe she hadn't noticed him?

"What did I do to you, Bell?" she whispered.

Bell hung his head. She was looking at him now, and he could see the tear tracks through the chapped skin of her cheeks.

"I'm sorry, Daelynn," he murmured.

"No you're not. If you were, you would've said so at recess. Or in class after. But no. I saw you with Parker. I didn't even think you two were friends!"

"We're not!" Bell growled.

Daelynn blinked. "Then why?"

Bell clutched at his notebook.

"I didn't mean it like that."

"Like what?"

"Like telling you to go away. I don't want that. It's just that I . . ." Bell cringed, his own tears tingling at the corners of his eyes. He took a deep breath. "I thought, you know . . . you'd be happier back home in Oregon."

Daelynn laughed, though Bell could tell she didn't think anything was funny.

"This *is* my home now. And you don't know!" she snapped. "You don't know me! And you didn't need to write that! You could have ignored that stupid paper, or torn it up like Ashi did, or taken it to Mrs. Vicker!"

Bell shook his head. "No. I've tried that stuff. Parker just takes it out on you later. I made the smart choice."

"To protect yourself, you mean? That doesn't make you smart. That makes you a coward, Bell Kirby."

Bell flinched like he'd been slapped. His stomach tightened, that bean seeming to push on everything, all at once. He tried to stop himself, tried to keep from fighting back, but the pressure was too much.

"Yeah, well at least I'm not a tryhard!" he snarled. He still didn't quite know what that meant, but if Tam had said it . . .

Daelynn stood up. Her face was crimson.

"A tryhard?! Yes! I am! I'm trying very, very hard! What else do you expect me to do? I had so many friends in Oregon! We rode horses, and we watched bad cartoons, and we'd laugh for hours. That's it! We'd just laugh at nothing, and it was the best!"

A dozen memories of Timmy and Bell doing the exact same thing, giggling randomly at the way a screwdriver fell off a table, or some guy burping at a restaurant, hit him, forcing his eyes down to the familiar view of his shoes. It didn't help.

"And now I have nothing! So sue me for trying hard to get even a little of that back! For hoping I might be able to find anything even remotely like that here! And you know . . ." She paused, coughing and sniffling. "You know what the stupidest part is? Huh? Do you know?"

Bell shook his head rapidly.

"The stupidest part was that I wanted to be *your* friend! Out of everyone!"

"M . . . me? Why?"

"I don't know! Maybe because you have a chinchilla and you draw and you helped me to music class on the first day? Does there need to be more than that?"

"I . . ."

"Well, joke's on me, isn't it? You're already friends with Parker Hellickson!"

Bell stood there, his mouth open. Before he could conjure the words to reply, a minivan pulled up behind him and honked. He jumped, dropping his notebook on the ground. He scrambled to pick it up, and by the time he had, Daelynn was sliding the door of the van closed. The bearded man in the driver's seat greeted her happily. As Bell watched, though, the man's face went from smile to concern, and Bell didn't need to be in the van to imagine what Daelynn was telling her dad. Not knowing what else to do, and not wanting to wait until the man looked at him, Bell clutched his notebook to his chest and ran.

Just like a coward would, he thought.

CHAPTER SEVENTEEN

Bell rolled his macaroni and cheese around with his fork, lumping it into little sticky towers on his plate. A green bean stuck in the top of each tower made pretty solid flagpoles. His mom had told him to eat his food three times already but had given up when she looked down at the playground of potato salad on her own plate. Eventually, she pushed it away entirely.

"All right, Bell, so let's talk," she said, her pinkie finding its way up to her teeth. It wasn't that there was anything stuck between them. His mom just picked at them when she was worried.

"Hmmm," Bell replied, moving a boulder of potato onto a green bean catapult.

"You think I don't know when something is up? I asked you how school was, and you went pale. Neither of us is leaving this table until I get some answers. Is it Parker?"

Bell nodded, and his mom exhaled sharply.

"God, I am so sick of this. Sick for you. Is it time to talk again about homeschool, baby?"

Bell cringed. "No, Mom!" he said loudly, and then, softer, "It's not like that."

"Why? What did he do?"

"He . . . he invited me over."

The clank as Mrs. Kirby's fork hit her plate was so loud it made Bell flinch.

"He . . ."

"Invited me over," Bell repeated. "To help with his Spring Festival float."

"Why?"

Bell shoved a forkful of macaroni into his mouth so he wouldn't have to answer right away. It was gummy and hard to swallow, but he wrangled it down.

After a sip of milk, Bell managed, "Tam told him I'm good at designing things."

It wasn't a lie, even though it felt like one. Still, it beat admitting that he'd helped Parker humiliate Daelynn, which was the first answer his brain screamed.

His mom wiped her lips with a paper towel, then twisted it in her hands.

"And you want to go down there?"

Bell nodded. "Parker's been . . ."

He was going to say "nicer," but he remembered Timmy's disbelief. So he went with, "Less mean lately."

"And you're okay with letting him use you for the float?"

Bell pouted. "Maybe he's trying to make up for . . ."

His mom lifted both eyebrows and tilted her head. Bell sighed.

"Yeah, okay. But Tam is going to be there. It could be all right."

"Well," Mrs. Kirby said, "if you think Parker's turned over a new leaf, and you think you're ready for this, then I guess I have just one more question."

Bell smiled. "Fire away."

"What time do we need to be there?"

Bell's smile disappeared faster than mac 'n' cheese in a garbage disposal.

"What? Wait, no, Mom. No 'we.'"

Mrs. Kirby laughed. "Joseph Bell Kirby, do you honestly expect me to let you go alone to the house of the boy who has tortured you for the last three years? You're the most brilliant eleven-year-old I know, but I'm not sure you've thought this one all the way through."

"If you're there, Mom, Parker will just—"

"Just keep his hands to himself? Just respect my son? Just be on his best behavior? Yes, I think I'm okay with all of that."

Bell gripped the edge of the table. His hands were sweaty.

He tried to decide which was worse: showing up with his mom to Parker's house, or telling Parker he couldn't come because his mom wouldn't let him.

In the end, it didn't matter, because his mom was already on the phone.

"Hello? Mr. Hellickson? Hi. It's Bell's mom."

"Mom, please . . . ," Bell whispered. She stared back at him, putting a finger to her lips.

"Actually, it's Major Kirby. Yes; no, that's all right. So yeah, Bell tells me that Parker has invited him over to help work on a float on Sunday. I thought, since our families haven't gotten together for so long, it might be fun if we brought along a cake or something. Would that be okay?"

Mrs. Kirby gritted her teeth as Mr. Hellickson responded. Bell held his hands up in a silent prayer.

"No, Captain Kirby can't join us. He's still stationed in Germany. And it'll just be Bell. I can't stay the whole time—I have to drop him off, then head to the workshop . . ."

His mom winked at him, and Bell heaved a sigh of relief. A drop-off he could handle. A babysitter would be mortifying.

"Yes, that's funny, Mr. Hellickson," Mrs. Kirby continued, "but I actually outrank my husband, so if anyone gave any orders, it'd be me. Fortunately, though, our family doesn't quite operate on army protocol . . . Don't worry about it. So we'll see you Sunday at three? Excellent. You too."

Mrs. Kirby hung up her phone and closed her eyes for a second. Her nostrils flared as she took a few deep breaths, and then she sat back down, grabbing her fork like a bayonet and stabbing a few unfortunate green beans.

"There you go, Bell," she said after a bite. "I'll drop you at Parker's house on Sunday."

"Thanks, Mom."

"Don't thank me yet. I've been hoping that you'd make it through this rough patch for a long time now, and if you really think your relationship with Parker is on the mend, then I'll support you. But I've still got my mom-radar up."

Bell nodded. "If things go bad, I'll call. I promise."

"You'd better," she replied, and she leaned over to kiss him on the forehead.

CHAPTER EIGHTEEN

The first things Bell noticed at Parker's house were the big rolls of chicken wire leaning against the garage. Right beside them was a pile of two-by-fours, and parked at the back of the driveway was a flatbed trailer. It seemed that Parker had grander plans than posters on a red wagon, and Bell's mind had already started piecing the wood together, draping it with chicken wire, and stuffing the links with colored paper. In the time it took them to walk from the sidewalk to Parker's back door, Bell had mentally constructed a crepe castle, a plywood praying mantis, and a rainbow unicorn.

He could have thought up more, too, but that last one sent a pang of guilt through his gut, and he stopped.

Mrs. Kirby had Bell knock, since she was holding a platter of chocolate cake. It was Mr. Hellickson himself who answered the door. He was tall, his mustache thin, and his hair was gelled into a permanent dark brown wave just like always. Still, Bell stared for a moment. It was odd to see Mr. Hellickson in anything other than one of those suits with the patches on the elbows. And shorts with sandals? In the middle of March?

Bell had to blink four times.

"Elise! Great to see you again," Mr. Hellickson exclaimed, and Mrs. Kirby was forced to quickly pass the cake to Bell so she could shake Mr. Hellickson's hand. Parker and Tam stood just behind Mr. Hellickson. As he stepped back, both boys skittered out of the way.

"And Bell," Mr. Hellickson continued as he ushered them inside. "I see Parker's finally decided to bring some brainpower into this! We both know he needs all the help he can get, right, buddy?"

Parker frowned. Mrs. Kirby said, "Oh, I'm sure these three will come up with a great plan in no time."

As Mr. Hellickson guided them into the kitchen, Bell scoped the place out. It was pretty much as he remembered, with a big bay window that overlooked the pool. Parker sat down at the table in the corner, and Tam reclined on one of the cushioned benches that ran underneath the window. Bell stood nearby, fidgeting with the hem of his jacket. He didn't join them until his mom delivered three plates of cake.

"Enjoy, boys," she said. "I have to head out, but Parker's dad . . ."

"Will be out in the garage!" Mr. Hellickson shouted

from the other room. Mrs. Kirby sighed straight through her smile.

"... In case you need anything—you know, like paper, or pencils, or—"

"More cake," Parker interrupted.

Mrs. Kirby nodded. "Yes, or more cake."

"Thanks for this, by the way," Tam said.

"Our pleasure, boys. Baking is one of Bell's favorite hobbies. He's quite good at it."

Bell smiled sheepishly.

"Wait," Parker spat, little crumbs of chocolate clinging to his lips. He stabbed his fork in the air at Bell. "You made this?"

"Yes, he did," Mrs. Kirby replied. Bell shot her a look.

"Dang! You should make more for our float party on the day of the festival! It's good!"

Bell felt the beginnings of a blush creep up his neck. "Float party?"

Parker had just shoveled another corner of cake into his mouth, so Tam interjected, "Yeah. Every year, Mr. Hellickson hosts a brunch on his lawn before the parade. Everyone brings their floats so that we can all start the parade together."

"My float's always the biggest," Parker proclaimed.

"I'm sure it is," Mrs. Kirby said, using the same voice she reserved for telemarketers offering her the credit card of her dreams. Bell had to stifle a snort.

"Anyway, we all get together out there on the front lawn. There's brunch and stuff for the grown-ups, and a big snack table for us."

"I didn't know that happened! We've always just taken Bell to the festival around noon."

"That's because Bell's never been invited," Parker said. Tam cleared his throat. Mrs. Kirby stared at him.

"I mean, this is the first year he's invited. You're totally invited, Bell."

"Thanks," Bell said quietly. "We'll come."

"Yes, we'll see you that morning. For now, though, I have to get going. Be good, boys," Mrs. Kirby said, and she slipped out the back door.

As he watched Parker wolf down the rest of his cake, Bell dragged his fork through his frosting, creating little wave patterns. It was Tam who eventually broke the silence.

"So the theme this year is . . ."

"Is dumb," Parker declared. Then he rolled his eyes and in a high-pitched voice said, "Village Green Elementary: Exploring Academic Frontiers."

Tam nodded. "The float has to be something with exploration, like space travel, or sailing to the New World. Stuff like that."

Bell stuck his frosting-covered fork into his mouth as he pondered. It felt good to have an assignment. After a couple of seconds, he popped the fork out and asked, "What do you have so far?"

"The supplies, and not much else," Tam admitted.

"Haven't you been working on this for weeks?"

Tam shrugged. "We were supposed to, but every time we came over, we ended up playing *FIFA* on Parker's PlayStation."

"Tam's just pissed that I kicked his butt four weeks in a row," Parker huffed.

"Whatever. Doesn't change the fact that we don't have much."

Parker snorted. "Sure we do! I've got a design!"

He stood up, fishing around in the pocket of his basketball shorts. He produced a piece of graph paper. Bell's eyes widened. It reminded him of the Woodja.

"This isn't the wagon thing, is it?" Tam sighed.

Yup.

It was the wagon thing.

At least, Bell thought it might be a wagon.

Or maybe a semitruck.

Whatever it was, Parker seemed quite proud. He slapped his drawing down on the table so hard the cake plates jumped, and he smoothed it out. Bell saw a brown box on wheels, with other boxes drawn around it. A giant stick figure sat at the front, holding onto a rope or whip, but the thing also had what appeared to be headlights.

And missile launchers.

"Is that Optimus Prime?" Bell guessed.

"That's what I thought at first, too," Tam said. "Or some kind of Transformer, at least."

"It's obviously a covered wagon," Parker snapped. "I just drew that other stuff in for fun."

"It's . . . it's not very Exploring Academic Frontier–y," Bell murmured after a moment.

"Sure it is! Big wagon, a pioneer just like the school mascot . . . I've even got a slogan: 'Driven to succeed.' Get it? Like driving a cart?"

"That actually is pretty clever," Tam conceded. Bell had to nod.

"See? It's brilliant. The wagon driver's arm is even going to move up and down while the float gets pulled."

"How are you going to manage that?" Bell asked.

Parker chuckled. "I have no clue. That's what you're for."

He leaned forward, staring at Bell hopefully. Greedily. Bell could even see the shadows of chocolate cake at the corners of Parker's twitching mouth.

"I . . . I guess you could add a belt to one of the cart axles, then cut a hole in the bed of the cart and feed the belt up and through. As the cart moved, the belt would spin, and that could operate a pulley that lifted and lowered the arm."

As he described his plans, Bell drew arrows around Parker's scribbled designs. He filled in precise measurements, angles, and materials. When he was done, he scratched the back of his neck and pushed away from the table.

"Kind of like that," he murmured.

"Awww yeah!" Parker exclaimed, and he poked Tam in the shoulder. "Your boy *is* a genius!"

When Parker got up to slap him on the back, Bell was surprised by the tingle of pride he felt. Parker had never, never complimented him on anything. And when they went into the living room to play *FIFA*, and Parker let Bell be on his team? That felt even better.

That all disappeared, though, when Parker got bored.

"So I heard Ashi convinced Daelynn to build a float, too," he said as he tossed his controller down on the carpet. The game was only half-over, but Tam set his controller down as well. Bell followed suit—apparently, when Parker was done, so was everyone else.

"Okay?" Tam said.

Parker grabbed a fish-shaped ashtray off the coffee table, leaned back, and started tossing it in the air, calmly catching it at the last second before it hit him in the face. It made Bell uncomfortable, because it looked like it was made of heavy glass. "Bell, you hate Daelynn. How stupid do you think her float will look?"

Bell felt a familiar knot in his stomach. He looked nervously at Tam, who gave him a little nod.

"Um . . . it'll probably be covered in horses," Bell mumbled.

Parker laughed. "I know, right? She's, like, obsessed or something. I wonder how bad she'd freak if we stuck pictures of dead horses in her desk. Or we could . . ."

To Bell's increasing misery, Parker kept up his plotting for ten minutes. He'd propose a way to hurt Daelynn, wait for Tam or Bell to laugh, nod, or agree, and then move on to the next idea. And if Bell wasn't quick enough to respond, Parker threw the ashtray his way, forcing Bell to fumble with the heavy thing before giving it back. By the time Tam heaved himself off the couch and announced he was going to get more cake, Bell's hands were trembling.

"Hey, get me another piece, too," Parker demanded, and he put the ashtray down. "I'm gonna start a new game."

"I'll get it for you," Bell said, and Parker smirked.

Once Bell was safely in the kitchen with Tam, he whispered, "Is he actually going to do those things?"

Tam ran a hand through his dark hair. "I don't know. Maybe. Most of the stuff he says he's going to do, he doesn't, but sometimes . . ."

"And you never tell him to stop? Or let someone know?"

Tam gritted his teeth and shrugged.

"But you're nice . . . I mean, not like Parker. How can you . . ."

"Because I don't want him on me again, okay?" Tam snarled. Bell's eyes went wide, and he shot a glance at the door into the living room. He could see Parker at the far end, untangling controller cords.

"Again?" Bell echoed.

"This is how it works," Tam hissed. He grabbed the cake knife and stabbed it through the frosting. "You want to be Parker's friend? You listen, and you laugh, and you get behind him, because it's a heck of a lot better than being the target standing in front of him."

Bell blinked. "Yeah, but we're talking about Daelynn. She's . . ."

"Not you, dude." Tam took a deep breath. Bell wasn't sure, but he thought he could even see tears in his friend's eyes. "And not me."

"You? But you've been Parker's friend since . . ."

"Second grade," Tam finished, and he scowled. "When Parker broke his toe."

Bell's cheeks went pink. He scratched slowly at his eyebrow, unable to look at Tam. "I . . . I did that."

"Oh, I know. Parker wouldn't shut up about it."

"I'm sorry."

Tam laughed, though it was clear he didn't think anything was funny. "Don't be. It was the best thing that happened to me all year."

"Why? Did you get Parker's starting spot or something?"

"It gave him a new target, okay? Before you, who do you think he picked on? If you guessed the new kid on his soccer team who juked him on the first day of practice, *ding*. You're a winner."

"I didn't know."

Tam let go of the knife. It was stuck in the cake, but it slowly began sinking toward the plate.

"Like I was going to tell you? 'Oh, hey, Bell, thanks for screwing things up with Parker, because now I can help him make fun of you instead of me.' See? You're the only reason my parents didn't pull me off the team, maybe even out of school. That's how bad it got."

Bell went pale. "You . . ."

"Sold you out? Yeah, basically. But since Daelynn decided to dump her chili in Parker's lap, you don't have to sweat it anymore, either. Enjoy," Tam grumbled, and he trudged back into the living room, leaving Bell to finish cutting a piece for Parker.

They spent the rest of the afternoon in silence—or, at least, Bell and Tam did. Parker talked his way through three more games and two more pieces of cake. Every other sentence seemed to be about Daelynn, each one meaner than the last, and neither Bell nor Tam said a word to stop him. By the time Bell's mom knocked on the back door, Bell was ready to run. He didn't say much of a good-bye to Parker, and he couldn't even bring himself to look at Tam.

At dinner, he answered every one of his mom's questions with "It was fine." He didn't make progress on the tank afterward, either, even when his mom said he could light Sir Weldmore on his own. And he couldn't fall asleep, no matter how much he tossed and turned. He tried calming down by remembering that he had survived an entire afternoon at Parker's and that Parker had even called him a genius, but that didn't work . . .

. . . mostly because when he tried to imagine it, all he could hear was, "That makes you a coward, Bell Kirby."

😊 Wow; this is late for you, Bell.

🔔 Yeah. Sorry.

😊 Early morning for us in Germany. I was just getting ready to take my *opfdäg*.

🔔 What's *opfdäg*?

😊 Not much, dawg . . . what's up with you?

🔔 Dad, please.

😊 Got it. No messing around this morning. Or evening. Or whenever it is. I take it this isn't about the puzzle, then?

🔔 No.

😊 And not just because you missed your dear old dad terribly?

🔔 Can I talk to you about something serious? Like, at school?

😊 Always, Bell. What's on your mind?

🔔 Things have gotten really weird. Parker's being nice to me.

😊 That's a bad thing?

🔔 It's because he thinks I hate a new girl at school, and he wants my help to make fun of her and stuff. If I help him, he's all friendly. If I tell him no, he'll go back to being the same old Parker again. Or maybe worse.

😊 What have you decided to do?

🔔 I don't know yet.

😊 If Parker is treating her like he's treated you in the past . . . you do know that's wrong, correct?

🔔 Yeah.

😊 Bell, listen. I know things haven't been easy the last few years. But I am so, so proud of the way you've adapted. Remember the talk we had with Mom, the one where we decided you'd avoid Parker?

Yeah. He's a pit of lava. To survive, you just come up with strategies to avoid the pit.

Exactly. And that doesn't mean Parker has won.

It just means I've changed the rules of the game. I remember.

Right. A bully doesn't win if he knocks you down. He doesn't win if he makes you cry. He doesn't even win if you try homeschooling in order to avoid him. That's just adaptation.

It doesn't feel like that.

I know, buddy, but getting up and running away? Crying? Telling a teacher? Making a system? Those are all responses. Those are all *something*, Bell. But when that bully acts in a way you know is wrong, that you know is unjust, and you do *nothing*? That's when he's won. He's made *you* more like *him*.

So what should I do?

Which is the right side? Parker's, or this girl's?

Hers.

Then I think you have your answer, buddy.

Okay.

Oh, and Bell?

Yeah?

One more thing: Sometimes, the best thing you can do for yourself? It's to stand up for someone else.

Okay, Dad. Thanks. I love you.

Love you too, Bell. Good luck.

CHAPTER NINETEEN

Bell's blond hair was cowlicked worse than usual, and he had dark circles under his eyes. As he sat at his desk, he held a trembling hand out in front of him. It felt like it was a hundred miles away, so impossibly far from his body that he had to reach out with the other hand to touch it, just to make sure it was there. In fact, his entire body felt floaty, and he wasn't sure he was going to be able to keep his breakfast down. Still, it was the best he'd felt in weeks, because at around two o'clock in the morning, that heaviness in his gut had started to shrink.

By 4:00 A.M., it felt no bigger than Timmy's bean.

And now? Here in homeroom? He couldn't feel it at all.

His black-covered notebook of systems sat upon his desk, and he ran a faraway finger over the spirals. Just beneath it, though, hid a new notebook, its cover green and glossy. It had taken his first all-nighter to make, but he had done it.

It was a thing of beauty.

Throughout math class, during those times that Bell could actually keep both eyes open at once, he watched Daelynn, trying to decide when might be the best time to talk to her.

He settled on lunch, and he tugged on her sleeve before she joined the cafeteria line.

"Daelynn," Bell whispered slowly. He found that he had to concentrate to make his tongue form syllables. It sounded funny, so he tried it again. "Day . . . Linnn."

"Leave me alone before I tell Mrs. Vicker," Daelynn growled, and she pulled her sleeve away.

Bell blinked rapidly. "Can we . . . can we talk?"

"No."

"Pleeeease? I'm going to be sorry . . ."

Daelynn crossed her arms. Bell shook his head to try to clear the cobwebs.

"Wait, no. That's not what I meant. I'm going to *say* sorry. For last week. For the Woodja."

"You already did. And then you went over to Parker's this weekend. I heard about it. So you can take your sorry and shove it."

Bell smiled, which only seemed to confuse Daelynn more.

"You're right!" Bell declared. "Totally right."

He glanced around, making sure Parker wasn't close by. Then he jogged to the end of the lunch table, set down his notebooks, and waved Daelynn over. She rolled her eyes but sat across from him.

"Okay, look," Bell started, leaning in. Daelynn cringed and slid back a few inches. Bell seemed not to notice. "I'm a bigger coward than you think. Because all this stuff Parker's doing to you? He's done it to me, for years."

Bell smiled again, this time with teeth. He pointed to his top right incisor. Chipped as it was, it looked a little like a vampire fang.

"See that? Drinking fountain, start of fourth grade."

Daelynn was silent, her arms still crossed.

"And the Woodja . . . that was, like, my third one . . ."

She scowled fiercely. Bell waved his hands.

"Oh, I was wrong. I get it. But that's the point. There is no *right*, because it's a trap. If I circle no, then Parker brings it up to you and says that I hate you. If I circle yes, then . . ."

Daelynn sniffled and looked toward the ceiling. "Let me guess . . . then he says you have a crush on me, and that would be, like, the worst thing in the world!"

"Yes!" Bell said. Daelynn pushed up from the table. "Wait . . . No! That's not what I meant. It wouldn't be terrible to have a crush on you. I mean, you're cool, and you do art things, and all the colors, and you like *The Wizard of Oz*, and . . ."

She sat back down slowly, her fingers pressed to her temples. "Are you trying to tell me you *do* have a crush on me? Because if so, this is a record-breakingly bad way of

143

doing it. We should call Guinness. They're gonna want to tape this."

Bell shook his head so hard it made him dizzy. Maybe staying up all night before trying to explain himself wasn't the best plan . . .

"No, Daelynn. What I'm saying is that it doesn't matter *what* Parker is saying about me, or about you. It just matters that he's saying stuff, because you know that once he starts, everyone else will pick up on it. And that, like, becomes your whole school year, right there. You don't remember your birthday party or the field trip to Kings Island or Creator Club. You remember Parker's voice, telling everyone your mom still wipes your butt. She doesn't, by the way. I take care of that myself now . . ."

"Thanks . . . for sharing?" Daelynn said, recoiling.

Bell blushed. "Sorry . . . I'm not saying this right . . . I'm a little tired . . ." He rubbed his fists against his eyes and looked around. More people were sitting at the lunch table now. How long would it be before Parker and Tam arrived?

Daelynn shrugged. "Actually, I get it. That's the way my year has started going, too. Except, you know . . . not with the wiping thing."

Bell nodded sheepishly.

"Still, though, it makes me mad, what you wrote. Especially since you knew all along what Parker was doing to me."

"You were right. I got scared. I'm a coward."

"Like the lion," she replied.

"Huh?"

"The Cowardly Lion. When he shows up in the movie, Dorothy bops him on the nose, and he gets all weepy. I guess I kind of bopped your nose when I yelled at you."

Bell reached up to rub the end of his nose, and Daelynn smiled. Then she said, "So, King of the Forest, what do we do about Parker?"

"Oh!" Bell exclaimed. "That's why I brought you over here. Look!"

He slid his own notebook to the side, revealing the green one beneath.

"Here. It's for you. I made it last night."

Daelynn took the notebook and opened it to the first page. Bell grinned, and his fingers shook as he pointed.

"That's your schedule—as much as I could remember, anyway. And that's Parker's. Now look at the next part. I made you a system! If you go by it, Parker won't be able to find you. It even tells you when and where you can get a drink of water, which seats you can sit in so that Parker won't be able get to you, and whether or not you can leave through the main doors in the afternoon on specific days."

Daelynn's brow knotted.

"I know it's confusing, but you'll get the hang of it," Bell continued. "Oh, and check out the next part. It's general tips. Lots of them I copied from my own notebook. Like this one: Keep your eyes low. Remember you teased me about looking down? I do it on purpose, since sometimes Parker won't bug you if you don't make eye contact. That's probably really important for you, because of, you know . . . the heterochromia."

Daelynn exhaled sharply. Using a finger to scan more of the tips, she read aloud: "'Number five: Wear gray or black. Blue jeans are okay, but not other colors. Don't wear shirts or hats that say stuff.'"

Bell nodded. "Yeah, that's a big one. In third grade, I wore a Cincinnati Cyclones hat to school. Parker took it and flushed it in the toilet. He said you were supposed to, to make it an official 'Cyclone.' I wore it for a whole day before my friend Timmy told me Parker was lying. I was pretty dumb back then, I guess. Do you have any blue jeans?"

"Yeah. I've got blue jeans, Bell," Daelynn said through clenched teeth.

"The last one is maybe the most important. Go on!" Bell insisted, rubbing his hands together.

"'Keep your hair one color,'" Daelynn read.

"Yeah. And don't get me wrong. I'm not saying you need to, like, run home and dye it brown tonight, but maybe you can just let it go back to its natural color . . ." Bell screwed up his face as he thought. "Is that . . . that's how hair dye works, right? Anyway, I know it's a lot, but you'll get used to it, I promise. What do you think?"

Daelynn closed the green notebook slowly. She pressed her hand to the cover, fingers spread. Then she stood up.

Bell grinned at her like a kindergartner presenting macaroni art.

"What do I think?" she echoed, leaning down so close Bell could see the individual colors of her braces' rubber bands. "What do I think? I think this stupid notebook is meaner than anything Parker's done to me. He might hate my hair, and my eyes, and whatever else, but at least he hasn't tried to *erase* me, Bell!"

Bell's jaw dropped. He watched as Daelynn closed her hand, crushing the cardboard cover before tearing it off entirely. Then she started ripping out pages, crumpling them up, too. Instinctively, Bell grabbed his own notebook, holding it against his stomach like a security blanket. When she was done, she had handfuls of shredded sheets, and the entire table of kids watched Daelynn scoop up all the wadded-up pages, march over to the trash bin, and dump them in.

As if she were suddenly aware of the audience—not to mention the three teachers who were hovering in "should we get involved" mode about ten feet away—Daelynn sniffled, straightened her jacket, and marched off.

A few seconds of silence settled in once she was gone. Then the cafeteria exploded with noise, every kid in there telling the others what they had just seen, even though every other kid had seen it, too. Bell looked for the exits so he could run.

A hand on his shoulder stopped him, though.

"Holy crap, Bell!" Parker exclaimed as he set his lunch

down. "That was epic! What did you just do to Daelynn? And why didn't you wait so I could see it, too?"

Justin slid his sandwich and milk into the spot Daelynn had used, and Tam settled in to Bell's left, boxing him in. He cowered as small as he could, but there was no escape.

"Seriously, man. What was that?" Justin said, slow-clapping as he spoke.

"I . . . I dunno," Bell mumbled.

"I've never seen her so mad! And I want all the details," Parker insisted.

Bell shook his head slowly, blinking back the sting at the corners of his eyes. Tam noticed and said, "Hey. I thought of a few things to add to our float . . ."

Bell heard none of them. He was too busy trying to figure out his mistake.

Because no matter how pleased Parker seemed, or how much Justin applauded, Bell knew one thing for certain.

His plan to help had been wrong.

Very, very wrong.

CHAPTER TWENTY

Bell found Daelynn in her usual spot after school, waiting for her dad to pick her up. A bunch of other students were milling around, too, while the dismissal monitors barked out bus numbers. Bell waited for a cluster of kids to pass, then plopped his backpack down in the grass next to her. She tensed but didn't run away, scream, or kick him.

All good signs, Bell thought.

"I was wrong," he admitted as he joined her. The ground was damp, and it seeped through his pants immediately. That's when he saw that she was sitting on a plastic bag.

"Just leave me alone, Bell."

He wrapped his arms around his legs and drew them up, resting his chin on his knees.

"I don't think I can," he replied.

She sniffled. "Why not? Because if you can't hurt me, you have no way to win Parker points?"

Bell cringed. "No. Because . . . because of this . . ."

Reaching into his backpack, Bell pulled out his note-book. Reverentially, he passed it to Daelynn. Her eyebrows knotted.

"Please don't tear it apart!" Bell pleaded. "It's not another plan for you. It's mine . . . my notebook."

She opened it slowly, tear-reddened eyes scanning the first page.

"I like the crocodile," she said after a few moments.

Bell blushed. "Thanks. He's . . . he's kind of my thing. He likes cookies."

"Who doesn't?" she replied, though she didn't look up.

"That route to music I showed you on your first day? That was my avoid-Parker-on-Thursday-mornings plan. It's one of my systems. I've . . . I've been using them for two years."

Now she did look up. "Two years?"

Bell nodded. "Parker's been on me for that long. Just like he's been on you. That's why I can't just leave you alone—I know exactly what you're going through, except for, um, the homeschooling part."

"What about it?"

Bell shivered. "My . . . my parents said they'd pull me out of school if things kept getting worse."

"Oh."

"And I'm scared."

Daelynn scooted a little closer. "I was, too, to come here. It's really, really different."

"And terrible," Bell guessed.

"Parker is terrible. Everything else is just . . . different. I haven't been able to figure out if things are good or bad, though, because when Parker's around, it all seems awful. Like I'm wrong just for being me."

Bell nodded. "I get it."

"But Parker likes you now, right?"

"That doesn't matter," Bell said quietly. "Because when I'm with him, *I* don't like me."

"You'd rather he hate you?"

"I've learned how to deal with *his* hate," Bell said, sweeping a hand over his notebook. "Yours? My own? Not so much."

Daelynn wiped at her nose with the back of her hand, then flipped the page. Bell watched as she read, her fingers tracing the drawings.

"Is this . . . is this a riddle?" she asked. Bell leaned over. She was looking at his dad's puzzle, along with the dozen or so designs he had drawn, then crossed out.

"Yeah. My dad and I like to mess around with brain teasers and stuff."

"What was the answer?"

"Dunno." Bell shrugged. "I haven't figured it out yet. Haven't had much time, to tell you the truth."

"Maybe I could try?"

Bell thought about what his dad had said: *a different perspective could help.*

"Sure, I guess."

"These are funny little pieces. They'll all fit together?"

Bell nodded. "Apparently."

"What do they make?"

Bell pointed to his father's explanation.

She read. "A bridge . . . that would be nice. That's all I want. A way forward."

"Me too. And I thought my systems could help us both."

She placed a hand across his spider web schedules. "It just seems so . . . exhausting. And to have to give up so much of who you are, just to avoid *him*?"

Bell shook his head. "No. I'm lucky. I like my systems. I'd probably have some even if Parker wasn't around."

Daelynn sighed, and she handed the notebook back to him. "I get it. This works for you. But not for me. I like my hair, and my clothes, and who I am. I don't want to change. I shouldn't have to."

"Yeah. I see that now."

Daelynn stood. Her dad had just turned the corner and was driving up the street.

"That's my ride. I've gotta go. But I accept your apology, Bell. And your offer. You want to help me? If you know what Parker's doing like you say you do, then *tell* someone about it. Be *brave*."

He wanted to explain that he had tried—so, so many times, and for years. But she was already at the van. Instead, he gently slid his notebook back into his bag and got up.

Before he could wipe the mud from the seat of his pants, though, he heard her. She had rolled the window down, and she stuck her head out.

"I'll think about that puzzle, too, Bell! Those pieces are strange, but they'll come together eventually. We'll get her across."

"That's the goal," he murmured, and he watched her drive away.

CHAPTER TWENTY-ONE

"Dude, that's just wrong."

Bell hunkered down on the floor of the tank, the wood creaking while the candles around him flickered. They had made incredible progress, his mom had said, and he had to agree: it honestly looked like da Vinci's tank, both outside and in. Sure, there was work still to be done; it didn't have a closing door yet, and they had another six hours of sanding to go before the inside wasn't a splinter waiting to happen. But for the most part, it was coming together well.

Unlike Bell's plans to help Daelynn.

"I know," he said to Timmy, who paused his sanding. He had been using two sheets of sandpaper at once, chanting, "Wax on . . . wax off . . . ," as he worked.

"Like, just because your system kept Parker off your back doesn't mean it's going to keep him off Daelynn's. Mostly because nobody's brain works like yours. You see a system like that, and you think, 'Sweet!' She sees it, and she thinks, 'Prison!'"

"I said I *know*," Bell growled. "She told me all about it. Very clear, on all points."

"Yeah. Ripping up your stuff and throwing it in the trash is pretty clear, I guess."

"Ya think?" Bell said.

"What would you have done, Tam?" Timmy asked. "You know Parker better than any of us."

"I'd do what I always do," Tam replied as he waved his hand over one of the candles. "Stay out of it. Like you should, Timmy. It's not like he bothers you."

Bell glared at him.

"That's 'cause he's not in my class," Timmy replied. "And because I'd just bite him. Guys don't mess with you if they know you're gonna go all honey badger on them."

Tam and Bell watched as Timmy started gnawing on his own arm. By the time he was done, there were little indentations all over his skin.

"What?" Timmy said, wrinkling his nose. "It works. And besides, Tam, tell me you don't get sick of seeing him do all this stuff."

"Maybe I do. I don't know. But why should it be my job to save Daelynn? It's not like she's some fairy-tale princess or something."

Timmy chuckled. "I think Bell gets that now."

Bell sighed. "Yeah, thanks . . . she doesn't need saving. But maybe that's not the point."

Tam yanked his hand back suddenly; he had held it too long over the flame. Rubbing at it, he said, "Then what is?"

"We know something bad is happening, and we're not saying anything. What kind of people does that make us?"

"You're saying we should tell on Parker . . . ," Tam said.

Bell nodded.

"Oh, like you did in third grade?" Timmy sighed. "Or fourth grade? Like, a billion times?"

Bell held up his hands. "Don't think I haven't thought about that. But what if it's the one billionth and first time that makes the difference?"

Tam shook his head. "Right. You're going to skip into Parker's dad's office and tell him his son is torturing the new kid."

"Well, I wouldn't skip . . . ," Bell retorted.

"I would!" Timmy declared.

"He won't believe you. And even if he did, he's not going to do anything about it," Tam said.

Timmy nodded. "That's true. The apple doesn't fall far from the tree."

Bell snorted. "More like that apple never fell. It's still clinging up there, all shriveled and rotten, and the worms are digging holes through it."

"*Ewww*," Timmy groaned appreciatively.

"You're not wrong," Tam added.

Bell stood up, wiping sawdust off his hands. He grabbed a piece of sandpaper from Timmy and ran his fingers along the roughness.

"Well, I've got to do something. Daelynn called me a coward, and it hurt more than anything Parker has said."

Timmy tilted his head, confused.

"Because it was true," Bell added.

Tam cracked his knuckles loudly. "So, what? Next time Parker does something, you tell on him?"

Bell stared back at Tam. "It's better than backing him up for years, I know that much."

Tam met his gaze for a moment but then looked away.

"Bean of the Spleen," Timmy murmured.

Bell nodded. "So unless you've got a better idea, that's the plan."

Timmy patted Bell on the back. "Knowing Parker, you won't have to wait very long . . ."

CHAPTER TWENTY-TWO

Bell didn't have to wait at all.

He and Timmy stood at the lockers. Timmy had a Rubik's Cube, and Bell was looking at his watch, timing Timmy to see how long it took him to solve it. The way Timmy's hands were flying, Bell thought he had a chance to break his record of thirty seconds. Just when Timmy was close, though, Parker stepped between them, Tam and Justin right behind.

"Bell, buddy . . . you're gonna love this," Parker said, glancing around to see if any teachers were nearby.

Timmy, who only came up to about Parker's shoulder, held the Rubik's Cube above Parker's head so Bell could still see. Parker scowled and batted it away like a buzzing fly. It flew out of Timmy's hands and hit the ground, forcing him to scurry after it.

"What?" Bell asked, though he couldn't help looking behind Parker, where Timmy had knelt down to get his cube. He had bared his teeth and was pretending he was going to bite the back of Parker's knee.

At least, Bell hoped he was pretending. He pressed a hand to his mouth.

"Stop yawning and listen," Parker continued. "I've been thinking about what you pulled off last week in the cafeteria . . ."

"I can't tell you what it was. I'm not even sure myself," Bell replied.

"Don't care," Parker said excitedly. "I just wanted to let you know: challenge accepted."

"Challenge?"

"Yeah. I've got something that will mess up Daelynn even worse than what you did!"

Bell's eyes widened. He looked at Tam, who gave a tiny nod. Bell swallowed, then said, "Really?"

Parker grinned, and he whispered, "I'm gonna—"

"You're gonna what?" Timmy interrupted as he stood up. Bell stared at Timmy, pursing his lips.

Parker's eyes narrowed. Then he turned back to Bell. "Actually . . . I'd rather not say. But you'll find out soon enough."

Justin laughed. "Yeah. It's gonna be hilarious!"

Bell rolled his eyes. Timmy mouthed, "What?" and then, when Bell jerked his head toward Parker, he mumbled, "Ohhh . . ."

As Parker and Justin headed into the classroom, Bell huddled with Tam and Timmy.

"You heard him. He's got something planned."

"Yeah, and he thinks he's in a competition with you to see who can hurt Daelynn more," Timmy grumbled, his fingers once again working at his Rubik's Cube.

"Everything is a competition to Parker," Tam said. "He likes winning."

"Even when nobody's playing a game?" Timmy wondered.

"To some people, it's always a game," Bell replied. "Easier to ignore people's feelings that way."

"That's deep, man," Timmy said.

"I didn't make it up. That's actually what Parker said to me in fourth grade after he tripped me going around the bases in kickball. 'If you won, you'd forget that you even fell down!'"

Tam nodded. "Yeah, that's pretty much Parker."

"So are you gonna tell Mrs. Vicker now?" Timmy asked.

"Tell her what?" Bell sighed. "We can't just walk up and say, 'Parker is plotting something!'"

"Why not? Tam and I could vouch for you; we heard it, too. And Tam probably knows all about it. Parker gives you all the inside info, right?"

"I didn't hear anything," Tam said, holding out his hands.

Bell rolled his eyes.

"What? Parker's my friend, too. I'm not going to get him

in trouble if he hasn't done something wrong. Like, I heard you talk about biting Parker just a couple days ago. Want me to go to your teacher and tell her Timmy Korver's planning to gnaw a kid's leg off?"

Timmy crossed his arms but didn't respond.

Bell said, "The best thing we can do is keep an eye on him."

"Well, good luck, man," Timmy said. "I've got to get to class myself."

As Timmy rushed across the hall, Bell and Tam slipped into Mrs. Vicker's room. Morning work had been passed out already, Mrs. Vicker was humming as she stapled spring poems to the bulletin board, and Daelynn was at her desk, like usual.

That's where the usual ended, though.

Bell wasn't quite sure where to look first; everything about Daelynn demanded to be stared at. Her usual red sneakers were gone, replaced by sequined silver boots that came almost all the way up to her knees. The pants were still there, but she had added more patches—robots, a chicken, crimson flowers, and a jack-o'-lantern, to name a few. She had taken off her moose coat, which let Bell see her shirt. It was black, except for a big triangle on the front. A ray of light shot through it and broke into a rainbow, so Bell recognized it as a prism. And her hair? She had spiked it and, from the look of it, probably re-dyed it over the weekend, since the colors were even brighter than before.

It was about as big a "To heck with your system, Bell Kirby" statement as she could make . . . well, except for actually tearing it up in front of him and throwing it in the trash. As he sat down, she looked at him and smiled.

That's fair, Bell thought, and he gave her a tiny nod.

CHAPTER TWENTY-THREE

I t didn't set alarms off for anyone else when Parker asked to go to the bathroom at 9:46, and certainly not for Mrs. Vicker, who let him go without a thought. But Bell knew better.

"Mrs. Vicker?" Bell said, raising his hand.

"Oh, Bell! You'd like to tell us more about the Mayan number system?"

"I need to go to the bathroom, too."

Mrs. Vicker rolled her eyes. "Yawning, vomiting, and kids needing to go to the bathroom . . . What are three things that spread like viruses, Mr. Trebek?"

"Huh?" Bell said, and the whole class laughed.

"Never mind. Your teacher is old and cranky. You can go as soon as Parker gets back. In the meantime, the Mayans?"

Bell peeled his eyes off the door long enough to glance at the board. Mrs. Vicker had drawn a series of lines and dots, stacked like pancakes with strawberries on top, and what seemed to be a seashell. Next to it, she had written "= 540."

After squinting at it for a few seconds, Bell said, "It's a base-twenty system. Dots are ones, lines are fives, and that little seashell thing is zero. Read them vertically and you'll get it." Then he looked back at the door.

"That's . . . that's right, Bell. Class, did you all follow that?"

Mrs. Vicker carried on, taking up the next ten minutes explaining exactly what Bell had just done in five seconds. Bell heard none of it. He was surer by the moment that whatever Parker had planned was going down now. Finally, unable to take it anymore, he raised his hand again. Just before Mrs. Vicker could call on him, though, Parker sauntered back in, a huge grin on his face.

"Oh, that's right, Bell! I'm so sorry! I almost forgot. You can head to the restroom now," Mrs. Vicker exclaimed.

"That's okay," he mumbled. "I don't have to go anymore."

She sighed. "Of course you don't."

When the class was dismissed for recess, Bell hung back, grabbing Tam before he could rush outside with the rest of the kids.

"You saw how long he was gone, right?" Bell whispered.

"Dude, I don't track how long it takes my friends to go to the bathroom. That's creepy."

"Oh, please. You know that wasn't what he was doing. We have to—"

A sudden, high-pitched scream cut Bell off. It had come from the hallway just outside their classroom.

"Wait here," Mrs. Vicker said, and she hustled out into the hall.

Bell looked at Tam for a half second, then followed Mrs. Vicker. Tam was right behind.

The hallway was mostly empty, so it was easy to see where the scream had come from.

Daelynn.

She was on her knees in front of her locker, and she was punching the metal doors so hard it echoed. Every few seconds, she stopped to sob, and it was during one of those pauses that Mrs. Vicker dropped beside her, wrapping her arms around Daelynn and holding her hands. Daelynn's knuckles were bloody.

"Stop, honey! You're hurting yourself!" Mrs. Vicker whispered. Daelynn clung to her.

Bell inched his way around, trying to get a glimpse into Daelynn's locker. When he did, he gasped.

Her sketchbook . . .

It lay open on the floor of the locker, and Bell could clearly see what had happened. On the two visible pages, someone had taken a thick black marker and drawn over every one of Daelynn's horses. Some were shot up with arrows or had their heads X'd out. Others had speech bubbles or thought clouds that said things like "Daelynn sucks!"

And some said far worse.

Bell's hands clenched into fists. For a moment, he wanted to punch something, too. But then Mrs. Vicker said, "Bell—the first aid kit under the sink. Get it, please."

As Bell rushed back into the classroom, he thought about his own notebook. A wave of panic hit him, and he veered from the sink to his desk. He grabbed his notebook, and he couldn't help but flip through the pages, sighing with relief when he saw that they were okay.

When he got back to the hallway, first aid kit in one hand and his notebook in the other, Timmy was there. He stood next to Tam, watching Daelynn cry. Bell handed Mrs. Vicker the first aid kit, and she carefully cleaned off Daelynn's hands and put Band-Aids on the scrapes. It calmed them all down a little to see their teacher being so gentle.

"What are you three still doing inside?" Mrs. Vicker asked once Daelynn had stopped shaking quite so badly.

"I was just looking for Bell and Tam, and then I saw . . . ," Timmy began, but he trailed off when he, too, spotted the sketchbook.

"Yeah," Tam said. "We were gonna meet up . . ."

"Well, move along, please. As you can see, Daelynn is very, very upset. I'm going to take her to Mr. Hellickson to get to the bottom of this."

Bell gripped his notebook in both hands, and he clenched his jaw. He glanced at Timmy, who nodded.

"Um . . . ," Bell started, his voice scratchy. Daelynn looked at him, her face a mess of tears. "Actually, I can take her, Mrs. Vicker. I . . . I have something to say to Mr. Hellickson about this."

Daelynn sniffled, and she sat up a little.

"What do you know, Bell Kirby?" Mrs. Vicker said sternly.

"I'd rather . . . rather tell Mr. Hellickson," he replied.

"Me too," Timmy added suddenly, his eyes going wide, like he'd surprised himself. "I've got stuff to say about this, too."

"And me," Tam said. "We'll all take her to Mr. Hellickson."

Bell stared incredulously at Tam. He shrugged.

Mrs. Vicker started to shake her head, but Daelynn stood up. She took the biggest, most trembly breath Bell had ever seen anyone take, and she blew it out slowly, almost like she was whistling. Then she rubbed her eyes, blinked, and said, "It's all right, Mrs. Vicker. I want them to go with me." Her voice sounded distant, as if she had been kicked out of her own body and was just now crawling back inside.

"Very well. We'll all go. You'll need to wait one moment—I have to call down and say I'll be late for recess duty," Mrs. Vicker stated, and she hurried back into the classroom.

"Thank you, ma'am," Daelynn said, and she reached into her locker, picking up her sketchbook like it was a wounded puppy. She wrapped her jacket around it and held it every bit as closely as Bell clutched his notebook. Then she turned, stepping unsteadily down the hallway toward the front office.

Bell looked at Timmy and Tam. They nodded, and together, they followed Daelynn, with Mrs. Vicker close behind.

CHAPTER TWENTY-FOUR

It was as if everything welcoming stopped past the frosted-glass doorway to the front office. Gone were the second graders' paper-plate flowers, the bulletin boards about Guatemala and Mexico, the math league trophy cases, and the scattered, brightly painted tracks of Readathon Rabbit. In their place hung framed portraits of uninhabited places, their skies all streaked with the same bruise-purple sunsets. Someone had printed a word beneath each scene, each one as meaningless as the next. What, Bell wondered, did a lake and some trees have to do with perseverance?

Mrs. Vicker had them wait while she talked to the secretary. Mr. Hellickson's assistant held up a long, rose-painted fingernail while she called back to the principal. Bell saw Daelynn grip her sketchbook a little tighter when the assistant said cheerfully, "He says you can leave them here; he's got it under control. We wouldn't want you to miss any more of your recess duty, Judith."

Mrs. Vicker stared pointedly at Daelynn. "Are you sure you're okay?"

Daelynn glanced toward Bell, Timmy, and Tam. Then she nodded. "We'll be all right," she said quietly. Mrs. Vicker reached down to take Daelynn's injured hand. She looked it over one more time, giving it a soft squeeze.

Then she left.

"You four can wait right in there." The secretary grinned, using that same fingernail to point into the waiting area outside Mr. Hellickson's office.

The four Trouble Chairs, as the students called them, sat along the wall next to Mr. Hellickson's door. Daelynn, Bell, and Tam squirmed in them while they waited. Even though they weren't in trouble, Timmy refused to sit in one, on principle. He sat cross-legged on the floor, picking at the carpet fibers.

"Stop fidgeting, Timmy, and get in a chair. You're making me nervous," Tam grumbled.

"Heck no. I've been at this school since first grade, and I've never had to sit in a Trouble Chair. Not gonna start now. You know moms can smell it on you, right?"

Bell snorted.

"Well, my mom probably could. I'd get home, and she'd be all like, 'Timmy! It smells like desperation, fear, and Australian buloke in here. Have you been sitting in a Trouble Chair?'"

"Australian buloke?" Tam asked skeptically.

"It's, like, the hardest wood there is. Look it up. Anyways, I figure that's what those chairs have to be made of, because they're so uncomfortable, right? It's supposed to remind you of the cold, hard concrete of a jail cell. That way, when you get into Mr. Hellickson's office, you're ready to spill your guts in the hopes that he'll be merciful."

"That's ridiculous," Tam said, but he slipped down to the floor. Bell joined them, and soon Daelynn did, too.

"I wish you were in our class," she said to Timmy. "You're funny."

He shimmied his shoulders a bit. "A'why thank you," he replied, and he sneered at Tam.

"No, thank you, guys."

"Thank Bell. He's the reason we're here," Tam said. "He said we needed to do something about Parker . . ." He trailed off for a moment, looking guiltily at the sketchbook Daelynn still held so closely. "And he was right."

"Oh, so now you're on our side?" Timmy huffed. Bell crossed his arms.

Tam glanced at Bell but dropped his eyes quickly. "It . . . it helped seeing that you guys were actually going to do it. I wasn't sure Bell could. I mean, I never did . . ."

Timmy wrinkled his nose in confusion, but Bell nodded, and he shifted his foot so that his sneaker softly tapped Tam's.

"Yes, Bell," Daelynn said. "I was . . . I was wrong. You're not the Cowardly Lion."

"Cowardly Lion? You mean, like, from music class?" Timmy asked.

Bell nodded. "Yeah, *The Wizard of Oz*."

"It's my favorite movie," Daelynn said.

"Actually, you *were* right. Dead-on," Bell admitted.

Tam nodded, and Daelynn said, "Well, I'm glad you're here. All of you."

They sat the rest of the time in silence. Daelynn forced herself to look through the whole sketchbook. Bell tried to peek over her shoulder, but some of the stuff Parker had drawn made him feel sick to his stomach—either because it was gross, or because of the way Daelynn reacted to seeing it. Tam fussed with his shoelaces, and Timmy kept picking at the carpet.

"Whoa, guys . . . check it out!" Timmy said, tugging at a particularly loose thread. It came up like a wriggly worm, a zigzag of gold and yellow carpet fibers that got longer and longer the more Timmy pulled. Soon, he had it stretched out above his head.

And then Mr. Hellickson's door opened.

Timmy jumped up, covering the pile of thread with his left foot. Tam stood, too, and Bell helped Daelynn to her feet, careful not to touch her Band-Aids.

"Looks like we're having a party out here!" Mr. Hellickson chuckled. He was wearing a suit. The tie was green and black—the school colors. "Bell, Tam—nice to see you again. And Mr. Korver as well! Mrs. Vicker called to say you were on your way."

"Daelynn's here, too, sir," Bell said.

"Well, of course she is," Mr. Hellickson replied, his smile broadening. "She's sort of a regular around here these days."

"We're here about—" Daelynn started, but Mr. Hellickson turned around before she could finish. He strode back into his office, beckoning them in with a sweep of his hand.

"C'mon in! There's only two seats, so you might want to bring a couple of those chairs to sit in."

"No thanks," Timmy replied. "I'm good with standing."

"Me too," Tam said.

In single file, they herded into Mr. Hellickson's office. Bell and Daelynn sat down, with Timmy and Tam behind them.

Bell had been here many times before, but it was never comfortable. Or comforting. The whole place was basically wallpapered with Village Green Elementary stuff. There were plaques and framed certificates of achievement dominating the walls, with more piled on the floor in rows three deep. Photos of previous principals, some black-and-white, hung behind Mr. Hellickson's desk, like they were all staring at whoever was across from him. That wasn't the creepiest part, however.

The Pioneer was.

Even though the Village Green Pioneers didn't have any sports teams, they still had a mascot. He was sort of like Daniel Boone—he even had a raccoon-skin cap—but he also had a big white beard and a bulbous nose. Bell thought he kind of looked like Grumpy, the dwarf from *Snow White* . . . only, somehow, meaner. He wore a green jacket and green pants, and in all the pictures, he held a long pole with the school flag on the end. It looked funky, and Bell knew why: in some of the old yearbooks in the library, the Pioneer was pictured carrying a rifle. They must have changed it to be more kid-friendly. Bell wished they would have changed his face, too, particularly with how it seemed to be staring at him now . . .

Hanging from a coatrack in the corner was a massive head. It was made of old felt, cotton balls, and enough hot glue to drown a giraffe. It was supposed to look like it was smiling, but the sides of its mouth had started to droop, so it seemed to Bell that it was gnashing its teeth as much as anything. Two great big black holes sat where its eyes should be, and its long gray beard was filled with grass and twigs from the Fall Festival hayride, which was the last time Mr. Hellickson had put on the costume. Propped next to it was the school flag, and beneath it swung the green jacket and pants, fringed and worn. Bell shuddered and looked away.

Mr. Hellickson pulled out his heavy leather chair and sat down. It squeaked as he leaned back.

"Mr. Hellickson, we're here—" Daelynn began, but Mr. Hellickson cut her off again.

"Wait, don't tell me," he said, pointing at Bell's notebook, then Daelynn's sketchbook. "You've brought some float plans, and you're excited to have me take a look. Parker told me you were building one. Bell, Tam, and Parker have been hard at work on theirs, too. Don't be worried if yours isn't quite as impressive, Daelynn. It's not a competition."

He held out a hand and snapped his fingers.

Bell said, "They're not float plans," and he nodded at Daelynn. She handed over her sketchbook.

Mr. Hellickson was still smiling as he opened it and began to look through. He even guffawed after seeing a drawing of one horse kicking another over a cliff. A few more pages in, though, he forced himself to look sterner, and he rubbed his finger and thumb over his mustache as he closed the sketchbook and put it on his desk.

"Well, I must say, you boys have vivid imaginations and art skills. But I'm surprised you'd show me this, what with some of the language I read in there. Not elementary school–appropriate at all. I'm afraid I'm going to have to—"

"It's my book," Daelynn said abruptly. "I drew most of it."

"Daelynn? I can't condone this kind of material—"

"That wasn't her," Bell insisted. He felt Mr. Hellickson's attention settle back on him, and he blushed. Still, he went on. "The horses and the fields, that's Daelynn. The blood and the violence and the bad words? That's Parker."

Mr. Hellickson's face pinched. "Parker? What do you mean?"

"It's true, Mr. Hellickson," Timmy said.

"Parker got into Daelynn's locker this morning and drew

all the bad stuff in there. He knew it would make her mad, because she worked so hard on it."

Mr. Hellickson's smile disappeared, and he leaned forward. Bell and Daelynn flinched as his elbows thumped onto his desk. Putting his fingertips together, he said, "And you saw him do this, Mr. Kirby?"

Bell frowned and shook his head.

"Daelynn? You witnessed him defacing your book of doodles?"

"They're not doodles. They're my art."

"Yeah, a doodle's like something you just whip up in the corner when math gets bor—" Timmy started, but Mr. Hellickson shushed him.

"Daelynn?"

Daelynn looked down, and she smoothed her hands over the line of patches on her pants.

"No, sir . . ."

"But we did hear him this morning, Mr. Hellickson," Bell managed, his voice cracking right on the "ick."

"Oh, Parker said he was going to do this? And you heard him? Tam, is that why you're here? You saw Parker? Or you heard your best friend say he was going to play this little trick on Daelynn?"

Tam gripped the back of Bell's chair. "No, Mr. Hellickson. I didn't see Parker do it, either. And Parker didn't say he was going to draw in her sketchbook."

Mr. Hellickson leaned back again, settling his hands into his lap. Bell swiveled in his seat to stare at Tam.

"But I did hear him say he was going to do something to Daelynn."

"His exact words were that he wanted to 'mess up Daelynn,'" Timmy added. "I heard him, too."

Mr. Hellickson pursed his lips. His mustache twitched.

"But none of you *saw* Parker do this."

Bell looked at Daelynn. Her shoulders slumped. Timmy rubbed the back of his neck, and Tam shoved his hands in his pockets.

"No," Daelynn said softly.

Mr. Hellickson took a deep breath, patted his hands on his desk, and stood.

"Daelynn? I'm very sorry that you're upset. But the accusation you're making . . . it just doesn't seem to make sense. First, the consequences for something like this—well, they might jeopardize Parker's standing on his AAU soccer team, and you know he'd never do that, Tam. And second, we've got the Spring Festival coming up. If anyone understands how important that event is, it's Parker. But quite frankly, I'm surprised by you, Bell Kirby, more than anything here. Parker's made real attempts to reach out, to help make you feel included, and this is how you repay him?"

Bell's mouth opened, but no words came out.

Mr. Hellickson slipped around his desk and opened his door.

"Thank you all for bringing this matter to my attention. Daelynn, you can leave the book, and I'll examine it further. As for Parker's involvement, I'll ask him about it tonight, but

I'm not going to pursue action against another student without conclusive proof of wrongdoing."

"What we said wasn't proof?" Timmy asked.

"If someone else came into my office, Mr. Korver, and told me that you had said something vague about wanting to hurt another student, and that student got hurt later in the day, wouldn't you want me to give you the benefit of the doubt?"

"Yes, sir," Timmy said, shooting a look at Tam. "But I'd totally understand if you dragged my butt in here to ask me about it, too."

Bell and Daelynn inhaled sharply. Tam shook his head and covered his face with his palm.

"Careful, Mr. Korver. You're on thin ice here. All of you . . . thin ice. If you actually witness something troubling, something worth my time, then please, do come back. Until then, though, I'm a busy man. And your recess is over."

CHAPTER TWENTY-FIVE

All four of them stood in the hallway, looking at the floor in awkward silence. It was Bell who eventually broke it.

"I'm kind of glad you didn't leave your sketchbook with him," he said.

Daelynn had slid it off Mr. Hellickson's desk on her way out, and had wrapped it back up in her jacket.

"Me too."

"Man, though . . . ," Timmy muttered. "If that sketchbook isn't proof of what a jerk Parker is . . ."

"Or all of us telling on him . . . ," Daelynn added.

"Then what kind of proof do we need?" Timmy wondered.

"More than that, obviously," Bell said as they started walking back to class. Recess was over, and kids were streaming into the hallway, forcing Bell to raise his voice. "I've tried to tell Mr. Hellickson about Parker a bunch of times. It goes just about the same."

"Does he ever get punished?"

Tam nodded. "Five bucks says he gets his video games taken away tonight."

"Even if Mr. Hellickson didn't believe us?"

Tam shrugged. "All I know is that his dad is on him a lot. And with the Spring Festival party coming up at their house? That's, like, Mr. Hellickson's big 'show off for the parents' thing. He warns Parker not to screw it up every time I'm over there."

Bell remembered Mr. Hellickson leaving them alone while he worked in the garage. It made him wonder how much of that float Parker would actually get to build.

"So what do I do now?" Daelynn asked.

"You mean what should *we* do," Bell said. "We're with you on this."

Daelynn rubbed a finger under her nose, then pushed up her glasses. "So we have a plan?"

Bell looked at Tam.

Tam looked at the ceiling.

Daelynn stared at both of them.

"Not yet . . . ," Bell admitted. "But we will!"

"We totally will," Tam added.

Daelynn nodded, shivered, and then laughed abruptly, her giggles punctuated by the occasional raspy sob. Tam jumped backward. Bell wasn't sure whether to comfort her or just let her carry on, so he hovered his hand over her left shoulder, patting the air.

"Um . . . there, there? It's all going to be okay?"

"I *am* okay," she replied. "For, like, the first time in months. My sketchbook gets trashed, my hand is all cut up, and I feel . . . hopeful?"

"Man, emotions are weird," Tam murmured.

"I know, right?" Daelynn said.

Bell shrugged, but as he thought about them—all four of them—in Mr. Hellickson's office, Daelynn's reaction started to make sense.

CHAPTER TWENTY-SIX

The rest of the day, Parker was impossible. He kept bugging Bell and Tam, asking if they'd seen Daelynn's reaction to her sketchbook. They both lied and said they'd missed it. More aggravating was the fact that no matter how much Bell tried, he couldn't get Parker to actually say he had ruined Daelynn's drawings. That was part of the problem: as good as Bell had gotten at navigating around Parker with his systems, Parker had the same amount of practice with not getting caught, so getting him to fess up was basically impossible.

But, Bell realized, they might not have to . . .

"You're gonna *what*?" Timmy asked from his perch on the armrest of Mrs. Kirby's recliner. Both boys had come over that evening as soon as they could.

"Get down from there," Bell hissed. "My mom's in the kitchen; she'll be back any second!"

Timmy slithered down to sit in the chair properly. Tam

and Bell were on their knees around the coffee table, staring at Parker's drawing of the float.

"Look, we need to get Mr. Hellickson to listen, right? As far as I can tell, there's only two ways to do that. Either get proof that Parker's bullying her—"

"Which we're not going to get," Tam grumbled.

"Or we've got to make a statement so big Parker can't ignore it," Bell concluded.

Timmy shook his head. "We already put our behinds on the line today in the office, and it did squat. What makes you think your new plan will work?"

"I thought the plan already worked! The tank looks *great*, guys," Mrs. Kirby said. Bell hastily shoved Parker's drawing beneath the tank sketches as his mom brought in a plate of marshmallow-swirl brownies. She gave each boy a paper towel with a brownie on top and a glass of milk. "Good idea to come over and celebrate finishing it last weekend, too. Mr. Randolph will be so stoked! I know I am!"

"Thanks for the brownies, Mrs. Kirby," Timmy said.

"Oh, don't thank me. I had to work in the garage all day. Bell made them from scratch when he got home from school. I just cut them up."

Tam and Timmy stared at Bell.

"What? I like baking. Preheating to three-fifty, sifting flour, whisking . . . it's a system."

Timmy grinned. "In that case, I want snickerdoodles for

lunch next Monday, key lime pie on Tuesday, Boston cream doughnuts on Wednesday . . ."

"Aaaand that's why I never told you I can bake."

"Oh, by the way," Mrs. Kirby said as she turned to leave. "I talked to Reggie at the scrapyard. He's fine with us borrowing his trailer to get the tank to school. I just need to let him know when we need it. The Creator Contest is in three weeks, right?"

"Yes, Mrs. Kirby," Tam replied.

"So how's about we take it in the weekend before? We can ask Mr. Randolph if we can store it in the gym or something; I doubt it's going to fit down the halls."

Bell shook his head. "Can't. That weekend is the float party at Mr. Hellickson's."

"That's right. I'm supposed to go to that, too, aren't I?"

"My mom and dad are coming," Timmy said, "mostly 'cause of the free food."

Mrs. Kirby winked. "Seems like a good reason to me," she said. "Anyway, the weekend sounds like a no go. I'll tell Reggie we'll get the trailer sometime early that next week, then, and we'll get the tank to Village Green after school on Thursday. Sound good?"

"Yup," Timmy said. Bell and Tam agreed as well.

"Good! Enjoy the celebratory brownies! Oh, and I can't *wait* to see everyone's reaction to that tank. It's going to be such a spectacle!"

As soon as she was gone, Timmy said, "Just so I have this straight, you're going to tell Parker off."

Bell nodded.

"To his face . . ."

Bell swallowed, but he nodded again.

"And you're going to do it, too?" Timmy asked Tam.

Tam took a deep breath, cleared a batch of bangs from his eyes, and murmured, "Yeah. We're not helping with his float anymore."

"Parker will be furious!" Timmy whispered.

Bell smiled gravely. "Especially when he hears what we're doing instead."

"Where Parker either gets so mad that he explodes, getting us the proof we need," Tam said.

"Proof Mr. Hellickson will have to deal with," Bell added.

"Or he at least sees we've got Daelynn's back and he stops messing with her? Man. That's intense." Timmy shuddered. "But what if Mr. Hellickson plays it cool again, and Parker just goes supernova later? Starts bullying both of you simultaneously?"

"He won't," Tam insisted. "He only goes after isolated kids."

Bell nodded. "And we're not isolated. Not anymore."

"True," Timmy said.

"Yup," Tam agreed.

"Then let's get to work," Bell said, and he opened his notebook to the next blank page.

CHAPTER TWENTY-SEVEN

"It's not what you think," Bell told Daelynn as he set a stack of papers on her desk. "Please don't, like, rip it up or anything."

She smiled, but her eyebrows dipped as she caught sight of the words "Daelynn's Schedule" at the top of the first page.

"Okay," Bell murmured, scratching at his cheek. "It's kind of what you think, but hear me out. That's a copy of all of our schedules—yours, mine, Tam's, and Timmy's. Not telling anyone where to go or what to do. Just for reference. So if you don't want to walk to gym class alone, you know where to find one of us. Or if Parker's giving you trouble, you can find backup quick. We . . . we sort of made a pact yesterday, and we were hoping you might want in."

"A pact?"

"Yeah. Nothing huge, but just to watch out for each other. Like, if you see Parker following me or something, I'd really appreciate it if you could run over and join me. We don't have to, you know, *talk* or anything. It'd just be a strength-in-numbers sort of deal."

"But we can talk if we want, right?"

Bell grinned, revealing his snaggly tooth. "Yeah. Of course."

"I'm in," Daelynn said. "But I doubt I'll be needing to protect you much. Parker doesn't pick on you anymore."

"Um . . . yeah . . . well, we'll see how long that lasts . . . ," Bell mumbled, and he scurried back to his seat before home-room started to fill.

Later, when Parker grabbed Bell and Tam and pulled them to the side at recess, Bell was sure Parker had found out about their plan. His face was that red, and he was stomping around that loudly. But when Parker thanked Bell instead of kicking him, he didn't know what to think.

"Thanks? For what?"

"For sticking up for me yesterday. You too, Tam."

Bell looked at Tam. He seemed just as clueless.

"My dad got a call last night from Daelynn's parents. She told them about her stupid book. He argued with them for, like, ever. I listened in to most of it. He told her parents that you were in his office yesterday, too, and you both said you didn't see me do anything, and you didn't hear me say I was going to mess with her drawings. Then he hangs up, and he gets in my face anyway. I say I didn't touch it, but he yells at me and takes my PlayStation away, 'as a warning.' I don't get my games back until after the school year is over!"

"That sucks," Tam offered.

"It totally sucks. And it's Daelynn's fault. The worst part, though, is that my dad's all like, 'I'm watching you, boy.' I can't even get her back for this. Not until later. We'll have to plan something this weekend when you guys come over to finish the float. I was thinking we could even . . . Hey . . . Guys? Are you listening?"

Bell wasn't, to be honest. His heart had started beating so hard he couldn't hear much else. When he looked down at his hands, he realized they were balled into fists, and he quickly slipped them behind his back. Tam was staring right at him, and Bell could see his Adam's apple bobbing in his throat and the tendons in his neck, all stiff. It looked like Tam might run away.

Don't run, Bell thought, though he wasn't sure if he was thinking it about Tam, or about himself.

"*Hello*? What are—"

"No," Bell squeaked. The sound of it made him cringe, and he realized he wasn't breathing. He tried to inhale, but it was like his lungs had been the first part of him to surrender.

"No? What 'no'?"

Parker Protocol . . . answer in short words. Stare at the mole, not the eyes . . . the eyes . . .

Bell looked up, straight into Parker's eyes.

"We're . . . we're not helping with the float."

"And we're not getting back at Daelynn," Tam added. The sound of his friend's voice opened Bell's lungs, and he took a deep, raspy breath.

Parker's gaze flicked over both of them, and his mouth curled. "This is a joke—"

"It's not a joke, man," Tam insisted, and he stepped up, shoulder to shoulder with Bell.

"What you did to Daelynn's sketchbook was wrong," Bell whispered.

Parker backed up a step. "Okay. I get it. You have a creepy obsession with notebooks. I can see how that might have triggered—"

"I don't think you do see," Tam said. "Leave her alone."

Bell crossed his arms in front of him. His hands were still in fists. "Leave *us* alone," he added.

Parker scowled, his lips twitching around words that wouldn't come.

His knuckles cracked as he curled his fingers closed, too. And then he left.

Tam and Bell watched him stalk across the field to Justin and Shipman. They watched his arms flail and feet stomp as he railed on, glad they weren't close enough to hear what Parker was saying. And when the bell rang, they found Timmy and Daelynn, and they all went back to class together.

The next day, Parker lingered outside the classroom after music, but Tam and Timmy were already standing there, and Bell and Daelynn joined them. At lunch on Thursday, Timmy sat at the table alone for a few moments, but Daelynn and Ashi parked themselves just a couple of seats away, and Daelynn didn't even start eating until Bell and Tam had flanked Timmy and settled in. And at the end of the day, they met outside Mrs. Vicker's room to walk together to Creator Club.

Once safely inside, Tam and Timmy went to score some snacks. Bell slipped over to Daelynn's workbench.

"Any trouble with Parker this afternoon?"

"No. I spotted Tam walking alone to art class, so I watched until he got there safely. That's about it, though."

"Thanks for looking out for him."

"It's weird, but it made me feel safer, too."

"I know what you mean," Bell said.

Daelynn noticed the notebook under his arm, and she reached up to tap its corner.

"Any luck on your dad's puzzle?"

Bell rolled his eyes and smiled. He flipped to a dog-eared section of the notebook, one with a cookie conveyor belt across the top, and he set it down so she could see.

"I like how you used the Lego piece in this one!" she whispered, pointing to a design. "Are those the sheep sitting on top of it?"

Bell shrugged. "I thought that if you turned it upside down, it might look like a mine cart . . ."

"And this ramp launches the cart across the water?"

"Yeah, but I couldn't figure out a way to build up enough momentum to get it going. Strike thirty-four."

Daelynn smiled. "Can I show you something, Bell?"

He glanced at the other end of her bench. Rachel and Chris were busy testing the different noises wire made when they dragged yarn across it . . . which meant they were ignoring Daelynn, like usual. Bell nodded, and she shifted a few papers off a stack in front of her. Buried beneath them was a thick spiral-bound pad.

"A new sketchbook?" Bell asked.

"Yep. I haven't shown anyone else yet, because . . ."

"I get it."

"Anyway," she said, "check it out."

When she pulled back the cover, Bell could only shake his head in wonder. The first page was a full-color illustration of da Vinci's viola organista, detailed down to the individual strings. Surrounding it was a halo of musical notes and symbols. The next page featured the piano-like organista on a stage, a girl wearing a tuxedo seated on a bench before it, ready to play.

"Those are amazing," he murmured.

"Thanks," she replied. "But that's not what I wanted to show you. I've been thinking about the puzzle, too . . ."

And then she showed him her designs.

Each one was sculpture-like, balanced and beautiful. None was functional, at least as far as Bell could see, but she had added color, shading, and the tiniest details. The crown had jewels. The faucet gleamed silver. And what he had interpreted as a spinning top, she had drawn as the arrow tip on a weather vane.

"What do they do?" he asked after a few moments.

"Nothing, really . . . ," she admitted. "But I thought maybe just playing around with them might spark some solutions."

"Decent plan. And sweet to look at, even if it doesn't work."

"Thanks," Daelynn replied, and she slipped her sketch-book back under the papers as Mr. Randolph came in and gave them their two-minute lights-out warning.

"Oh, one more thing," Bell said. "We heard you and Ashi were building a float for the Spring Festival parade."

Daelynn sighed. "Trying to. Saturday is our last opportunity to work on it, and I think our idea is a little too out there."

Bell glanced over at his bench, where Timmy and Tam had built a soccer goal out of carrot sticks. Tam was aiming a cherry tomato between the posts, and Timmy crouched at the end of the table, his mouth open and tongue out.

Bell took his own notebook back and turned to join them. Before he left, though, he asked, "What if you had some help?"

Servicechat.Army.Gov   **Connected**

How's school? Were you able to figure out the thing with Parker?

We hope so.

We?

Yeah. Timmy, Tam, and I.

And the girl?

Yeah.

I bet she appreciated the support.

I think so.

But?

But what?

I can tell when you're worried about something. I can see it in your eyes.

You can't see my eyes at all. You're in Germany.

Or I'm RIGHT BEHIND YOU.

Dad . . .

You looked, didn't you?

No.

Suuuuuuure you didn't.

I didn't.

Yeah, okay. We'll just say you did and move on.

Fine.

HA! I knew you did. Anyway, you were about to tell me what's bothering you.

I guess I'm worried about Parker still. Tam and I were supposed to go to his house tomorrow to help finish his float. But we backed out.

I see no reason why he shouldn't respect that decision.

We kind of agreed to help Daelynn with hers instead.

Ah. And you're afraid that will upset him?

Oh, I'm pretty sure it will.

Do me a favor, bud. Tell your mom that you're worried. She likes to know what's going on with you, and there's nobody in the world who wants to help more. Or, at least, nobody on your continent.

I'd rather not.

I could tell her instead . . .

No!

Gonna make getting a ride to Daelynn's pretty tough if you don't talk to Mom . . .

Sigh. I will, I guess. I love you, Dad.

Love you, Bell!

CHAPTER TWENTY-EIGHT

On Friday night, Mrs. Kirby found Bell sitting in the middle of his room, a bunch of PVC tubes and chinchilla toys surrounding him. Fuzzgig was on his shoulder, alternating between staring down at Bell's hands and nibbling him playfully on the ear.

"What'cha working on, Bell?" his mom asked as she closed the door carefully behind her.

"I'm trying to open up Fuzzgig's house a little. You know, give him a bit more breathing room."

"He's no bigger than a softball. How much room does he need?"

Bell shrugged. Fuzzgig hopped down, bounding by to sniff at Mrs. Kirby's feet. He nipped her sock quickly. Then he spotted the empty paper towel tube Bell had set down, and he ran over to shove his head into it. Mrs. Kirby rolled her eyes.

"Little weirdo."

"I think he's funny," Bell replied defensively. Fuzzgig stumbled around a bit, rammed his tube-head into Bell's hip, then used his forepaws to shove the thing off... Whereupon he blinked a couple of times, chewed a little piece off the tube, and promptly crammed his head in again.

"I wasn't talking about Fuzzgig," Mrs. Kirby joked. Bell stuck his tongue out at her.

"See, though, Mom?" Bell pointed. "It's like I give him all these tubes to climb in, passageways to explore, and places to hide, and he's never happier than when he's just running around on my bedroom floor."

Mrs. Kirby sat down on Bell's bed, ducking to avoid hitting her head on the top bunk, which was covered in pieces of robotics kits and model airplanes. She grabbed Bell's pillow and put it across her lap.

"That's the way of some things," she said. "Structure isn't for everyone. Heck, your father and I thank our lucky stars every day that we had a kid who craves it."

"I know, I know," Bell sighed. Doing his best Mom voice, he added, "'Our little Baby Bell settled into his sleep schedule before he was a month old, drank exactly twenty-five ounces of milk a day, and even needed his diaper changed at the same times. We called him our clockwork kid!'"

"Oh, good. You've been listening to me brag about you all these years."

Bell yanked the tube off Fuzzgig's face. He got nipped on the knee for his troubles, so he gave it back.

Mrs. Kirby smoothed her hands over Bell's pillow. "It's a good thing, too. Your father and I . . . we're pretty much the same way. I'd be lying if I said it wasn't a big reason we joined the army. But it's also a reason lots of people can't picture themselves in the military, and that's okay, too. Like little furball here. He'd make an awful field commander."

As if in reply, Fuzzgig bolted under the desk, the tube still on his head. They heard an echoey thunk, and then the chinchilla reappeared, tubeless and looking slightly dazed.

"See what I mean? Systems aren't for everybody."

Bell smiled.

"Yeah, I know a few people like that."

"Maybe that's why you're nervous about tomorrow?"

Bell looked down at his hands. "You can tell?"

Mrs. Kirby surveyed the mess around her son.

"Call it mother's intuition . . . Anyway, I know if I was as used to avoiding Parker Hellickson as you are, I'd still be a little hesitant to want to go work with him."

Bell fit together two pieces of clear plastic pipe, twisting to lock them together.

"Actually," he said, wringing his hands along the pipe joint, "I'm not going to Parker's."

Mrs. Kirby leaned forward, hugging the pillow in her lap. "Oh?"

Bell put the pipe down. Fuzzgig darted in, sniffed once,

then skittered back under the desk. Bell held his hand above the opening so that he at least got a drive-by snuggle.

"He's been . . . bad lately."

"How bad?" Mrs. Kirby said, her brow furrowing.

Bell took a deep breath, closed his eyes, and then told her. He thought she was going to rip straight through the pillow when he got to the part about Daelynn's sketchbook, but she seemed to calm a bit when he described their new approach.

"Why didn't you tell me about this before?" she asked once Bell had finished.

Bell felt a sting in his eyes, and he brought his knees up to his chest.

"I don't want to be homeschooled."

Mrs. Kirby smiled softly, and she pushed back a few blond curls. Then she slipped off the bed to join Bell on the floor.

"That was always up to you, Bell. We'd never pull you out of school unless we had your blessing."

"I didn't want to hurt your feelings, though."

"Why, because you thought I'd be mad if my eleven-year-old son didn't want to spend every waking moment of his life with his dear old mom?" She grinned and reached out to tousle Bell's hair. He scooted away and wrinkled his nose.

"So you're not mad?"

Mrs. Kirby snagged Bell's ankle and reeled him in for

a hug, holding him until he got fidgety. "Not at all. I'm proud of you. And I think you're very brave, Bell. I'd think so even if you wanted to be homeschooled. It's not an easy decision."

"Daelynn was homeschooled. She liked it."

"Lots of kids do. But let me tell you, it's not sitting and watching TV all day. Or fooling around in the garage."

Bell nodded. "I know."

"Well, if it's not for you, it's not for you. And I won't bring it up again unless you do."

"Thanks, Mom."

Mrs. Kirby stood up. "Is there anything else I can help with? Except cleaning this mess up. You're on your own for that."

"Actually," Bell said, "yeah. Can I get a ride to Daelynn's house tomorrow morning? Tam, Timmy, and I are going to help her and Ashi with their float."

"Her address is in the online directory, I assume?"

Bell nodded.

"Buster, you've got your ride," Mrs. Kirby declared. "And until then, I'll leave you to it. Bedtime is in an hour."

"I'll be done by then," Bell assured her.

When she was gone, Bell finished repairing Fuzzgig's habitat, and he lured the chinchilla back in with a raisin. Then he watched as Fuzzgig zipped through the new pipe arrangement once, only to settle back into his usual spot, staring out at the floor of Bell's bedroom. It made Bell wonder about the last few days and how he didn't have a procedure to deal with all the changes. He almost grabbed his notebook to design a new system.

But then he thought about Daelynn, Timmy, and Tam, and he realized he already had one.

CHAPTER TWENTY-NINE

Bell wasn't sure what he thought Daelynn's house would look like. A rainbow-colored roof, maybe? A barn in the back? But it was just like all the other houses on her block: two stories, a nice front porch, and a one-car garage. It did have bright red shutters. They reminded Bell of Daelynn's shoes.

Bell waited in the car with his mom until Timmy and Tam showed up. Once they did, he joined them on the lawn. Daelynn's dad must have been looking out for them, because he opened the front door and waved. Daelynn and Ashi were behind him.

"Dang," Timmy said when he saw Mr. Gower. "He's all regular-parenty. I was hopin' he'd have, like, a nose ring or something."

"Maybe he has his belly button pierced. You could go ask," Bell replied.

"Seriously? 'Cause I'll bet it's like a pirate skull or something, wedged in there and—"

Tam rolled his eyes. "No, not seriously. What's wrong with you?"

"I hang out with too many strange people," Timmy shot back.

"Guys . . . ," Bell warned when they reached the steps.

"C'mon in, boys!" Mr. Gower said, and he stepped out to hold the screen door open. "We've got some snacks set up in the family room, but you'll be working out back. Sorry about the boxes. We've been a little slow unpacking."

Daelynn met them just inside. She had a rope of red licorice hanging from her mouth like a farmer's piece of straw, and she wore a pair of plaid PJ pants rather than her usual patchy ones. Her feet were bare, and Bell could see the silvers and golds she had used to paint her toenails.

"Dad," Daelynn said, speaking clearly despite the licorice, "this is Bell, and that's Timmy and Tam. They're in Creator Club with me."

"Very nice to meet you," Mr. Gower said. "I think I've seen Bell before."

Bell blushed. "Yes, sir. I wait after Club with Daelynn sometimes."

"Hey, guys," Ashi said, and she pointed to the room to her left. "We're in here."

Mr. Gower clapped his hands. "I'll leave you to it! I'll be in the kitchen if you need me. Daelynn's mom is at work."

"On a Saturday?" Timmy asked.

"Don't start," Tam murmured.

As they followed Daelynn into the family room, Bell snuck a look at the pictures on the walls. Some of the paintings looked old—landscapes, mostly, but there were a few photographs as well. One was of Mr. and Mrs. Gower on their wedding day. It was in black and white. Mr. Gower looked happy, and Daelynn's mom did, too. Even though she had longer hair than Daelynn, Bell could see the resemblance.

In the family room, Timmy had also picked up a photo from a line of them on a bookshelf. It was framed in purple and had seashells pasted around the outside.

"Hey, you look normal in this picture!" he said.

Bell froze, and Tam shook his head.

Timmy pointed to the image. Daelynn was on the right, holding the bridle of a chestnut-brown horse. Standing next to her were three other girls, each clutching the reins of another horse and beaming proudly. Daelynn wore a plain white shirt and riding pants, and her hair was about the same color as Bell's. It was much longer, too, and nearly reached her waist.

Daelynn smiled wistfully and eased the picture out of Timmy's hands. "That's Isabelle, Camryn, and Liu. They're my friends back in Oregon."

"The ones from the stable," Bell ventured.

"Yeah," Daelynn said. "They threw me a going-away party. We dyed our hair each other's favorite colors. You know, so that we'd remember . . ."

"That sounds like fun," Ashi replied.

"And also normal," Tam added, shooting a look at Timmy.

"I just meant—you know . . ." He turned to Daelynn. "The way you dress and all."

"I like giving people something to talk about when they see me. That's always been my thing."

"Oh, like the stuff on the walls at Cracker Barrel," Timmy said, nodding.

Bell put a hand on Timmy's shoulder. "We're sorry. We don't take him out very often."

Daelynn laughed. "It's fine. Do you guys want something to eat before we get started? We have candy, chips, and grapes. Careful, though. I think they might still have seeds."

The snack bowls were arranged on top of a brown box that served as a makeshift table. The actual table in the room was just under the window, and it was covered with porcelain houses, each one painted meticulously, down to the flowers on each bush. Another box sat on the floor beneath, its lid open wide and a bunch of newspaper wadded up inside like a nest.

"That's our idea," Daelynn said as Bell stared down into the box. "Well, not *that*, but the newspaper. We had so much left over from the move that we thought we'd make something out of it."

"Like stuffing?" Tam asked.

"More like papier-mâché," Ashi replied. "We were a bit scared to try it, since we thought it'd make a mess."

"A huge mess," Daelynn agreed.

"Did it?" Timmy asked.

Daelynn and Ashi shared a grin. "Oh yeah. And that's been the best part!"

"What are you trying to make?" Bell asked, and he picked up a crumpled piece of newspaper. He smoothed it out. It was the front page of an *Oregonian* from 2016.

"Well," Daelynn said, "you know the theme?"

"Yeah," Tam replied. "Exploring Academic Frontiers."

"We thought we'd do a hot air balloon. Ashi's mom had this huge exercise ball that she wasn't using . . ."

"Yeah, it's bigger than me," Ashi confirmed.

". . . And so we've been putting layers of torn-up newspaper on it for the past few weekends, then letting them dry."

Tam nodded. "What have you been using to bind it? Paste?"

"Water and flour," Ashi said.

"That works, too."

Daelynn grabbed another piece of licorice. "We're mostly done, except for painting it. What we don't have is a basket for beneath . . ."

"Or a way to hold up the balloon . . . ," Ashi added.

"Or some way to get it moving," Daelynn finished.

"So you basically have a ball covered in newspaper at this point," Bell said.

Daelynn and Ashi nodded sheepishly. Bell glanced at Tam and Timmy. They smiled.

"We can work with that."

After finishing their snack, the four members of Creator Club and Ashi headed through the kitchen to get to the backyard. Mr. Gower was enjoying a mug of tea by the back window, and he assured them that he could see them just fine as they worked. Bell paused to compliment him on the setup: unlike the family room, the kitchen was completely unpacked, and it reminded him of their garage at home. Gleaming copper pots and pans hung from hooks in the center of the kitchen, almost like they were floating above the granite-topped island in the center. A massive rack of spices hung near the refrigerator, and one of the windows was shaded by sprigs of drying herbs.

"Do you like to cook, Bell?" Mr. Gower asked as Bell marveled.

"I bake, mostly," Bell replied.

Daelynn's dad curled his hands around his mug, his thick gold wedding ring tapping against the ceramic. "Well, we'll have to have you and your parents over to try out a few recipes one of these days. This kitchen is just itching to be put through its paces."

Bell smiled. "That'd be great."

"Oh, and one more thing."

Bell paused, his hand on the doorknob.

"Thank you."

"Sir?"

"Daelynn is a sharer," he said, swirling his tea slowly and

letting the steam rise. "Always has been. And she's told us a great deal about you—including how you've tried to make school a little more hospitable for her. We were worried that we'd made a mistake in sending her to Village Green."

Bell glanced outside. "I don't think you did."

"We're starting to feel the same way," Mr. Gower replied, and he waved Bell off with a grin. "You can go on. Don't want to keep you from the project!"

"Okay," Bell said, and he hustled down the back steps to join his friends.

In the center of the yard, Daelynn and Ashi had set up two lawn chairs, pushing them together to create a holder for the exercise ball. They pulled a tarp off it to reveal their work so far. It was more than Bell had anticipated; they had even added ridges of newspaper and a curl below so that it looked like an actual hot air balloon—one that read like the last forty back issues of *The Oregonian*, but still . . .

"We have paint and stuff in the garage," Daelynn declared. "And a pretty good woodpile, too. Whoever owned this house before us must have liked building fires in the winter."

Timmy grabbed Tam by the sleeve. "We'll check that out."

"And I'll help get the paint," Bell added.

It took the five of them nearly all day to finish, but by the time they were done, Mr. Gower was applauding underneath the porch lights. Fully eight feet tall when put together, the balloon had a basket big enough for Daelynn or Timmy to sit in. That's where Timmy was, even though the paint hadn't really dried yet above him; sky blues and grass greens were dripping into his hair, but he didn't seem to mind. Tam and Ashi continued to fiddle with the handles—they needed to be secure so that whoever was pushing the float could keep it going straight, since the wheels they had screwed into the bottom tended to veer the whole thing to the left. Daelynn and Bell sat in the grass, looking up at the balloon itself. It sat on four supports, around which Ashi had wound yarn so that they looked like real ropes. Each one of them had painted a part of it, and Bell thought it was the best horse-dragonfly-velociraptor-ankylosaur-styracosaurus mash-up he'd ever seen.

"The Spring Festival party is at Parker's house, isn't it . . . ," Daelynn said softly.

"Yeah," Bell replied.

"What do you think he'll say when he sees this?"

"I hope he doesn't say anything at all."

"Is that possible?"

Bell shrugged. "Well, it's bigger than his float, so . . ."

Daelynn smiled. "Let him talk. As long as we're there together, we'll be okay."

"True," Bell said. "Now, let's get Timmy out of the basket before he falls and takes the balloon down with him."

Daelynn giggled, and they stood up to help their friend. Together, Bell, Timmy, Tam, Ashi, and Daelynn took great care in cleaning up, securing their float, and making sure it was protected against the weather. As they did, none of them realized that their efforts didn't matter.

After all, their float would never leave Daelynn's backyard.

CHAPTER THIRTY

On the morning of the Spring Festival, Bell awoke to the sound of Fuzzgig spinning in his wheel. He slid out of bed, and even though his mind was racing as fast as his chinchilla, he forced himself to go through his routines: Take a shower. Get dressed. Give Fuzzgig his pellets and hay. Eat his own breakfast. Brush his teeth. He treated it like any other Saturday.

Even though it definitely wasn't.

"Beautiful day for the parade!" Mrs. Kirby said as they stepped outside. Bell had to agree. It was still chilly in the shade, but if he stood in the sunny patches between the trees, he could feel the warmth on his forehead and in his cheeks, whispering that summer was on the way. The flowers in his mom's garden had started to pop through the soil, and the entire neighborhood was the light green of new leaves. It seemed to Bell that there was a buzz in the air, made of more than just bees and early cicadas, like a fuse was sizzling down to an explosion of change.

He knew the feeling.

Cars already lined the street leading down the hill. Some of them Bell recognized, including Timmy's parents' Honda and Tam's dad's SUV. He looked for Daelynn's dad's minivan but didn't see it. And once Parker's house came into view, he stopped looking at the street anyway.

Dozens of parents were setting up tables and chairs or bringing food to the heavy table set up along the driveway. Some kids played soccer off to the side, while others sat near their floats, making final tweaks and adjustments. Bell grinned: Timmy had been right. Most of them were wagons with posters hanging off the sides. A few, though, were more substantial, and none bigger than Parker's.

In the center of the lawn was the flatbed, and Bell had to admit that Parker and his friends—or, more likely, their parents—had done an impressive job. The wagon sported actual wooden wheels like in a cowboy movie, and the covering looked to be made of honest-to-goodness leather. In the driver's seat was the Pioneer himself, all green and bearded. Mr. Hellickson must have brought him home from school to use as the centerpiece of their float.

As his mom strolled over to put the chocolate-chip cookies he had baked on one of the snack tables, Bell looked for Timmy and Tam. He spotted Timmy next to his parents, who were chatting with Mr. Randolph. He slipped in next to them.

"I'm sure they've been hard at it, Mrs. Korver," Mr. Randolph said appreciatively. When he noticed Bell, he tipped his baseball cap. "And there's the architect now!"

"Bell!" Timmy exclaimed. He wiped a hand across his forehead.

"Hey, Bell!" Mr. Korver said. He held out a big hand for Bell to shake. "We were just saying that Timmy's been over to your place so much to work on your Creator Club project that we're going to have to have you over one of these days."

His mom smiled. "Quid pro quo, as they say."

Timmy nodded as he grabbed Bell's arm. "That's Latin for 'you're invited to come over to my place for a sleepover next weekend. Bring brownies.'"

Mr. Randolph laughed, and he leaned in to Timmy's parents.

"Don't worry. They offer Latin classes in the middle school."

As they continued talking, Timmy dragged Bell underneath the huge oak tree near the driveway.

"Man, what took you so long? I've been here sweating bullets!"

"I had to go through my systems. Otherwise I'd be so nervous I'd still be in bed."

"Well, how's about *our* system? Have you seen Daelynn yet?"

Bell looked around again. Still no sign of her.

"Maybe she's just having trouble getting the balloon into her dad's van," Timmy whispered. "It's awfully big."

"We measured it. With the seats down, it should fit."

"Still, she should be here by now," Timmy said, and he shielded his eyes from the sun as he scanned the yard. "Ashi's over there by the snacks. Let's ask her if she's heard from Dae."

Bell followed Timmy to the snack table, but the parents setting up shooed them away. Ashi didn't know anything about Daelynn either, but she seemed just as worried as Bell and Timmy. They were forced to pass the time wandering around Parker's front yard, avoiding soccer games and Parker himself. Every so often, Bell glanced toward the street, looking for a familiar spike of rainbow hair.

It was just as they started letting kids swarm over the snacks that he spotted her.

"Daelynn's here," he told Timmy, and he pointed. She was with her dad, and they were walking hand in hand over to Ashi's parents. Mr. Gower looked tired.

Daelynn looked furious.

"We should go check in with her," Bell suggested.

Before they could make it even halfway across the yard, though, they were interrupted. "Bell! There you are!" Parker shouted. He ran up to them, his soccer ball tucked under his arm, clumps of grass in his cleats.

"You wore your cleats to play in your front yard?" Timmy asked.

Parker ignored him. "Rough weather last night, huh, Bell . . . ," he said. Shipman, huffing and sporting grass stains on his knees, stumbled up to join him.

"Weather?" Bell wondered, and he kicked at the ground. Other than a bit of dew on the grass, it was dry.

"Yeah!" Shipman wheezed, "Big . . . storm . . ."

"Lots of rain, I heard," Parker added with a sneer.

Tam, who had just arrived, jogged toward them. When Parker spotted him, he threw his soccer ball away and chased after it, Shipman groaning as he tried to keep up.

"Trouble?" Tam asked.

"Maybe," Bell said. "It didn't rain near you last night, did it?"

Tam shook his head. "Dude, it hasn't rained in Cincinnati for over a week."

Timmy gritted his teeth. "Then yeah. Trouble."

Together, they maneuvered their way around a few more floats, including a cardboard rocket ship, a bike with wings meant to look like the Wright Flyer, and a go-kart covered with dozens of Ohio State logos. Timmy paused at that last one, asking the kid what it had to do with exploration or frontiers. The fourth grader responded by screaming, "Go Buckeyes!" at the top of his lungs.

"All right, bro. You do you," Timmy muttered, and he scampered to catch up with Bell and Tam, who had found Mr. Gower.

"I am so, so sorry, boys," Daelynn's dad said, running a hand down his beard and shaking his head. "I was sure we had the tarp on there, but this morning, well, our neighbor's sprinkler started up, and I guess they must have moved it near the property line, because . . ."

He trailed off as Daelynn and Ashi marched up.

"It's ruined," Daelynn spat. Her eyes were red and puffy, and her voice cracked when she spoke.

"I'll admit, I suggested we not come at all, but Daelynn insisted she be here for you," Mr. Gower said, wrapping an arm around Daelynn's shoulders. She sighed raggedly, then closed her eyes and pressed her cheek to his ribs.

"Thanks," Timmy offered.

"Yeah," Tam said.

"It'd be cool if you stayed," Bell added. "Even though . . ."

"Do you want to stay, Lynnie?" Mr. Gower asked softly.

Daelynn sniffled and nodded, gently easing her father's arm away. "I'm okay," she whispered.

"Um, if you want," Bell said, "my mom is over there near the driveway, Mr. Gower. You could say hi."

He nodded and thrust his hands into his pockets. "Think I'll do that, and I'll explain what happened to the float. You guys just try to enjoy yourselves."

"Thanks, Daddy," Daelynn said, and she took a deep breath.

When he was gone, Timmy growled, "Oh, I know what happened to the float. Bad weather, my butt."

Ashi arched an eyebrow.

"Parker," Bell said. He could feel his chest tightening as soon as he spoke, and he realized his hands were shaking. "He just came up to us, talking about storms and rain. Daelynn, he *knew*."

"Probably because he did it," Tam sighed. "It doesn't take a genius to figure out where you live, rip off a tarp, and move a sprinkler."

"And, yet again, we have no proof."

"And no float," Daelynn muttered. Ashi flumped on the ground and started picking at the grass dejectedly.

"So, what, he wins again?" Timmy asked. "He can just do stuff like this to us anytime he wants?"

"No," Bell whispered, his head down. "He doesn't win."

"Um, yeah, he does," Tam countered. "Not only does Parker get to rub this in our faces, but he gets to do it while riding down the street on his giant float."

"Ours is bigger," Bell mumbled.

"Was," Ashi sighed. "It's a melty pile of newspaper and paint-mud now."

"No, ours *is* bigger."

Tam threw up his hands. "What are you talking about, Bell? Our balloon is ruined, and it's not like we're going to be able to just make a new float right now, let alone one bigger than Parker's. For starters, you'd need something huge, like a tractor or a pickup or a monster truck, or . . ."

Bell lifted his head. His brow was furrowed, and his nostrils flared.

Through clenched teeth, he said, "Or a tank?"

CHAPTER THIRTY-ONE

"This is a stupid idea," Tam warned as he scrambled to keep up with Bell.

"This . . . is . . . an . . . awesome . . . idea!" Timmy panted from behind them.

Bell marched on, legs burning as he climbed the hill. He had told his mom he wanted to get something from home—not exactly a lie. And when she saw that Tam and Timmy were going, too, she said it was fine.

"I'm telling you, your mom's gonna kill you, Bell," Tam warned.

Bell stopped, catching his breath.

"Yeah. She'll be mad. And that will suck. But it won't be as bad as knowing Parker's going to continue being Parker. He will, too. You know it."

Tam grimaced.

"C'mon, Tam. Are you seriously gonna say you don't feel guilty when Parker hurts people? Even though you were his friend, and you could have probably told him to stop?" Timmy asked.

Tam sighed, scratching the back of his neck. He glanced at Bell, then looked down at his shoes. "I've felt guilty for the past two years," he said softly.

Bell raised a hand to block the sun so he could look at his friend, and he smiled.

"So you're saying you're in?"

Tam shrugged.

"I'm here, aren't I?"

"Sweet!" Timmy said, rubbing his hands together.

"I still think it's a stupid idea. And even if your mom doesn't kill us, my parents will."

"I dunno," Timmy countered. "It's about time Creator Club had a float. And we've gotta get the tank to school for the contest anyway, right? Might as well save Bell's mom a trip!"

Tam looked as if he was going to argue more, but he saw the gleam in Timmy's eye, and he shook his head. "Keep walking, Korver," he grumbled.

Bell continued his way up the hill, pointing out mailboxes and garbage cans, bumps in the sidewalk and dips in driveways, anything that might cause problems.

"It's a good thing it's pretty much a straight shot down to Parker's," Timmy observed once they reached Bell's house. "I don't know if we could handle a U-turn."

Bell took a deep breath. "I don't know that we can handle

a turn at all. Once it gets moving down the hill, it'll be all we can do to direct it a little to the left or right. Then we'll have to ease it to a stop with the other floats."

"That's when I get to pop out and scream, 'You lose, Parker!'"

Tam grabbed Timmy by the shoulder. "Please don't."

"Awww . . ."

Bell shook his head. "No. The goal is just to be there. To show him we won't back down. And who knows? Maybe it'll make Parker mad enough to blow up."

"Mr. Hellickson can't ignore us then, not with all the parents there to see," Tam concluded.

"Who's driving?" Timmy asked.

"You mean who's doing lookout?" Tam replied. "There is no steering wheel . . ."

"I will," Bell said.

"I want left wheels!" Timmy exclaimed.

"Guess that means I'm right," Tam muttered.

"Good. Now we just need equipment. Bike helmets are in the front closet," Bell said. "And bungee cords are in the basement, in a big brown box under the stairs."

"Bungee cords? What do we need those for?" Tam asked.

"For the pillows," Bell said. Tam screwed up his face, but Bell had already started hoisting the garage door. The tank dominated the space, and Bell took a moment to run his hand along the sanded-smooth planks. He thought about what they were planning to do—how upset his mom would probably be. But he also thought about Daelynn, and about Parker, and about how this felt like the most important thing he'd ever done. Or maybe would ever do.

Timmy returned first, letting the bike helmets fall to the concrete with a satisfying series of hollow pops. He joined Bell in looking up at the tank and touching it reverently.

"You know what I bet, Bell?" Timmy said.

"What?"

"I bet that no matter what, Parker leaves us alone after this."

Bell smiled helplessly. "And why's that?"

Timmy patted the sloped side of the tank. "'Cause we're gonna be the guys who built a tank from scratch, rolled it down the street, and parked it on his front lawn. Would *you* want to mess with us?"

Bell laughed, and he turned to hug his friend. That's when he saw that Timmy was wearing his mom's huge welding goggles. It made him look like a grasshopper.

"Yeah, um—" Bell started, but then Tam returned, the box of bungee cords in his hands and a pile of pillows on top. Bell grabbed two cords and two pillows and immediately made a sandwich of himself, putting one pillow on his back and another on his chest, then wrapping the bungees around until they were held snugly in place. Slipping his bike helmet on, he turned to face his friends.

"Timmy, take the goggles off," Tam said. "You look ridiculous."

Bell cleared his throat. "I . . . um . . . think he'll be okay."

Timmy and Tam turned to stare at Bell. Tam's jaw dropped. Timmy fell to the floor laughing.

"It's like . . . like a sumo wrestler rolled around in glue, did a belly flop into a pool of tissues, 'n' then decided he'd like to go for a little bicycle ride afterward!" Timmy said, pointing up and snorting.

"A marshmallow, dude. Just say he looks like a marshmallow," Tam huffed. "And what are you doing on the floor? Nothing's that funny."

Timmy stood up, brushing himself off. "Burning off some of that nervous energy, you know? Besides, it's not my fault I'm surrounded by people with no imagination. And I'm keeping the goggles, by the way."

Bell shrugged, then helped Tam and Timmy with their pillow armor. Once their cushions were snugly in place and their helmets tightened, they turned to look at their engineering masterpiece one final time.

"I hope we don't make Mr. Randolph too mad," Tam said.

"I hope we make da Vinci proud," Bell added.

"I hope we go over a big bump, get some air beneath us!" Timmy whispered.

All three boys nodded gravely. Then they climbed in.

Bell positioned himself at the front peephole and peered out. He could see quite a bit—all the way down the driveway and out to the street. He knew this first step was likely to be the trickiest—they'd have to take the tank straight, then get it turned ninety degrees to head down the hill. By his calculation, Tam would need to start rotating his wheels backward right about at the midway point of the driveway. It meant they'd have to shear through part of his mom's garden, likely crushing a few tulips and daisies on the way. It was unfortunate, but Bell figured that replanting them was something he'd have time to do once he was grounded for life.

Bell glanced down at his shaking hands and took a deep breath. Then he looked back at his friends. Tam gripped his crank bar tightly. Timmy gave him a double thumbs-up. Bell nodded and then said, "Go."

Timmy whooped, and Tam groaned as he started twisting the bar. Bell spun around to look out the peephole, his hands pressed to the wood on either side.

They didn't move.

"It's stuck!" Timmy whined.

"Mine too," Tam said, rubbing his sore hands together and flexing his fingers.

"It's too heavy. I should have figured. We're . . ." Bell paused, thinking for a moment. "We're gonna have to push from behind."

"You mean get out? Like my mom and dad had to do when our car ran out of gas last year?"

Bell nodded. "We'll keep the door open. Once it starts

rolling, we can jump in and hopefully guide it by controlling the crank bars."

"Hopefully?" Tam repeated nervously.

Together, they lined up behind the tank. Bell and Tam leaned their backs against the low roof. Timmy, between them, put both of his hands on the edge, then shoved his helmet against it for good measure.

Then they pushed.

At first, nothing happened, except a lot of grunting and sneakers squeaking on the concrete. But then, slowly, the tank started to crawl forward. It stopped whenever any one of the boys had to change positions, but if all three were straining simultaneously, it moved.

And when it got to the gentle downward grade of the driveway, it began to roll on its own.

"Get in!" Bell shouted, and Tam sprinted around to hop inside. Timmy used his pillows to do a belly flop, and the other two dragged him the rest of the way in. The tank was still only inching forward, but the two cranks were spinning on their own, and they could feel it slowly picking up speed.

"Tam! Slow your crank down!" Bell instructed, returning to his position at the front. Tam grabbed his crank with both hands and braced his feet against the inner wall. The crank slowed, and so did his wheels.

The tank began to turn to the right.

"That's it! It's turning!" Bell exclaimed. "Nice brake

work!" His heart felt like it was beating a billion times a minute.

"Lemme see!" Timmy said, and he shoved his goggles right up against the peephole.

"Get back to your crank!" Tam yelled. "There's no way I can control this thing on my own!"

"Sorry! Sorry," Timmy said, and he jumped back into position.

Inexorably, gravity pulled the tank along, the wheels first crackling, then thundering along the asphalt of the driveway. Everything went quiet, though, when the front wheels slid off the pavement and into the soft soil of the garden.

The tank began to slow.

"Push!" Bell said, and he slid back to help Timmy. He could actually feel the wheels wanting to bog down. He growled as he pushed his entire body against the crank, willing it to keep spinning. Tam had stood up and was lifting his crank like a bodybuilder.

The tank slowed down even more.

But it didn't stop.

The crunch of concrete beneath them once more meant they had reached the sidewalk, and all three cheered. Properly on the hill now, they started picking up speed quickly. Bell rushed back to the peephole and began directing his friends.

"Timmy, ease up just a bit. Tam, keep going steady . . ."

"What?" Tam yelled. "I can't hear you!"

Tam was right. The noise the tank made as it rolled was deafening.

Quickly, Bell came up with a system of hand gestures, and his friends caught on. He held up a fist when he wanted them to slow their wheels, and he pointed when he wanted them to spin. By the time they were midway down the hill, Bell was beaming, a wild rush of euphoria replacing all his nerves, all his frustrations, all his fear.

He was *driving* a *tank*.

Until, quite suddenly, he wasn't.

"Uh, Bell?" he heard Tam shout.

"Yeah, Bell?" Timmy yelled.

Bell turned around. He saw his two friends huddled near the back of the tank, as far away as they could get from their cranks.

And with good reason.

They had reached critical speed, Bell realized—the cranks were spinning so fast that Tam and Timmy couldn't hold them anymore. That meant they couldn't slow down. They couldn't steer.

They couldn't stop.

"You guys are supposed to be the brakes!" Bell screamed. Covering his ears against the noise, Bell looked out the peephole once more. Parker's front yard was in sight. Most of the people were frozen, staring straight at the massive, domed monstrosity rolling down the hill. Daelynn, though, was all motion. She begged, pleaded, and pushed people to get them to back up. That had been her job: making sure that nobody was in the way. And nobody was . . .

. . . mostly because they weren't aimed anywhere near Parker's house, Bell realized with a gulp. They were still shooting down the hill as straight as an arrow, the tank keeping to the sidewalk. If it continued on that trajectory, it would fly right past Parker's house.

Past the floats.

Past Parker, and Daelynn, and his mom.

And into the street.

Desperately, Bell calculated. By his estimation, they had to get the tank to turn slightly to the right, slicing off the sidewalk and into the grass ahead of Parker's driveway. Maybe, just maybe, that would slow them down like his mom's garden had. But there was no way he could grab the whirring crank; even trying would probably break both his arms. His eyes darted over the entire mechanism—the central rod, the welded corners, the interlocking spokes of the spinning gears, clattering and chewing together like teeth.

Like teeth . . .

"Marshmallows!" Bell yelled suddenly.

"What?" Tam screamed back.

Bell didn't respond. Instead, he unclipped his bungee cords, taking his pillows off. One of them was from his bed—the same one his mom had held the week before. Giving them a solemn squeeze, his entire body shaking from the tremors of the tank, he fed them to the machine.

Instantly, the sound of shredding fabric joined the gravelly grinding of the wheels on the pavement. Feathers filled the inside of the tank, blinding Bell and his friends. There was a fraction of a second when the front right wheel seemed to choke on the pillow, too much of the stuffing cramming between its connection with the crank rod.

The right side stalled briefly.

Bell gasped, scrambling to get back to the peephole. When he looked out, he no longer saw sidewalk. Instead, he saw Parker's front yard. He saw people staring, their mouths open and fingers pointing. And he saw Parker's float, tall and proud, the dark eyes of the Pioneer seeming to leer at him.

They were headed straight for it.

Of course, they'd have to get through the snack table first.

Bell fell to the floor, the tank rattling his rib cage as he braced for impact. Timmy and Tam grabbed each other, curling into a tight ball. The grinding of the wheels on the pavement gave way to the hiss of surging through grass, and then they heard a spectacular crash as the tank took out the snack table.

If it slowed them down, though, Bell couldn't feel it.

In fact, they were still going at top speed when the tank rammed Parker's float. Timmy and Tam were thrown forward, rolling along the floor to crash into Bell, who was smashed against the wall, his helmet cracking hard against the boards. The noise was catastrophic—the screech of the wheels, the splintering of wood and squealing of twisting chicken wire, and then a thunderous thump as something outside fell.

And then everything got quiet.

Bell sat up and shook his head. His ears were ringing, but otherwise, he seemed okay.

"Would you get off of me?" he heard Tam bark, and he pushed Timmy away.

Timmy rolled onto his backside. When he took his helmet off, its shape was indented into his hair.

"Did . . . did we make it?"

Bell and Tam nodded slowly, and all three of them helped one another to the door. They opened it and stepped out, like aliens appearing from a flying saucer.

Bell blinked, letting his eyes adjust. It had been much darker inside the tank. When he could see, he slipped his helmet off to look around. A warm breeze blew through his blond cowlicks, and it felt good.

A ring of people had surrounded them. Inside that halo, it was a disaster area. Scraps of wood and leather were everywhere, and the lawn had two parallel sets of tank tracks gouged across it. Behind them, they had left a wake of paper plates, napkins, potato chips, and cookies. The snack table lay in a mangled heap off to the side. And in front of them was Parker's float.

Or what was left of it.

The tank's low rim had lodged itself beneath the trailer,

which had slid up the sloped side of the armoring like it was climbing a steep hill. The weight of the Pioneer, the wagon, and all the decorations must have then dragged it over, because it had flipped upside down, landing about ten feet away. It was wheels-up, and one of them was even still spinning. The only things relatively unharmed were the Pioneer's legs, which poked out from beneath the trailer at a funky angle.

That brief moment as everyone stared at the carnage was one of the most peaceful of Bell's life. It ended quickly, though. An explosion of noise and movement enveloped him as his mother rushed forward, grabbing him and pulling him in close. Tam's and Timmy's parents were right behind her, and then it was all chaos. His mom started yelling at him.

Mr. Hellickson started yelling at him.

Parker? Oh, he was absolutely yelling at him.

But Bell didn't really hear any of it. He was staring at Daelynn, who was chewing her purple-and-black-painted nails and shrugging helplessly. If their goal had been to give Parker something to fume about, well, they had certainly done that. But Daelynn had been wrong, he realized as he scanned the destruction around him. They weren't the Cowardly Lion, or the Tin Man, or the Scarecrow, or any of them.

No.

They were the tornado.

Mom told me what you did.

Sorry.

You endangered yourself and destroyed Parker's property, Bell. I don't think "sorry" covers it.

I know.

She also told me why. I'm disappointed that you couldn't think of another way to stand up for Daelynn.

We tried . . .

But I'm proud of you for doing it.

Does that mean I'm not in trouble?

Ha. HA. HAHAHAHAHAHAno. You're in a ton of trouble.

Oh.

You have a meeting on Monday with Mr. Hellickson, right?

Yeah.

Whatever he says the consequences are? You agree.

Okay.

And that's just the start.

I know. Mom said. We ruined Mr. Hellickson's flatbed and his table.

Exactly. What are you going to do about that?

I don't know. Apologize to him?

Do better.

How?

I've heard our garage has a lot of empty space these days.

🍪 Yeah. Ohhhhh is right. Kiss your evenings and weekends good-bye.

🔔 Ohhhhh.

🔔 That's heavy.

🍪 That's a start. Mom will let you know more, including how you're going to become real, real familiar with advanced gardening techniques this summer. Her bulbs ain't gonna replant themselves.

🔔 I understand.

🍪 Good. Now go to bed without any supper.

🔔 It's nine in the morning here, Dad.

🍪 Sucks to be you.

🔔 Dad!

🍪 I love you, Bell.

🔔 I love you too, Dad. Sorry.

🍪 Good night.

🔔 Dad . . .

CHAPTER THIRTY-TWO

B ell didn't have to worry about his system at school on Monday morning, because his day started in Mr. Hellickson's office. He sat in one of the uncomfortable chairs, his head down, Timmy and Tam to either side of him. It had been twenty minutes of yelling already, their parents all crowded into the little room around them while Mr. Hellickson pounded on his desk.

"And if I'm being honest," Mr. Hellickson spat, "at least some of the blame here lies with you, Mrs. Kirby! Allowing three eleven-year-old boys to build such a thing. Of course they're going to have the poor judgment to try to use it!"

"Hey! That's a stereotype!" Timmy squeaked.

"You hush," his mother hissed, smacking him on the shoulder.

"'K. But still," he muttered.

Mr. Nguyen said, "Let us at least be grateful that nobody got hurt."

"Nobody got hurt? Nobody?" Mr. Hellickson shouted. "My boy spent all day yesterday sulking in his room! Do you have any idea how hard he worked on that float? How hard *I* worked?"

"We know," Bell's mom said, struggling to keep her voice even. "That's one of the things Bell's father and I stressed in our conversation yesterday, and it's why he's willing to accept whatever consequences the school deems appropriate."

"The same for Timmy," Mr. Korver added.

"Likewise," Tam's mother agreed.

"Oh, there will be consequences, all right. All that damage, and for what? Showing off their ridiculous contraption?"

"It wasn't ridiculous," Tam mumbled. "It worked."

Mr. Hellickson raised a finger, but Bell interrupted him.

"And we weren't showing off," he said softly. "We were speaking up."

"That's absurd!"

Bell looked to his left and right. Timmy and Tam nodded slowly.

His mom cleared her throat. "Go on, Bell. Tell him what you told me."

After taking a deep breath, Bell said, "Parker."

Mr. Hellickson's eyes went wide.

"Are you saying this was meant as an attack on my boy?"

Bell shook his head. "No. It was meant to stop him from attacking Daelynn."

And then Bell and his friends explained it all, from the morning Daelynn arrived, through the Woodja and Bell's apology and Daelynn's sketchbook. The parents grumbled behind him when he described their earlier meeting in Mr. Hellickson's office, and they gasped as the boys revealed Parker's destruction of their own float.

"And that's why he told us there was a hurricane," Timmy said.

"Rough weather," Bell corrected.

"Oh yeah. Rough weather. My bad."

"That's preposterous," Mr. Hellickson huffed.

"We didn't say it was a *good* prank," Bell whispered.

"The very idea of it is nonsense, just like the notion that Parker defaced that girl's drawings. There's simply no proof—"

"Are you calling my son a liar?" Timmy's dad said.

"And mine?" Tam's dad added.

Mrs. Kirby crossed her arms. "Mr. Hellickson . . . George. I've been in your office, what, seven, eight times over the past three years? And every time, it's been to have a tense conversation about the things your son was doing to mine. Bell comes home with his shins all bruised. You say it's just rough play in gym. Fine. He doubles up on knee-high socks before the next PE class. He shows up with a chipped tooth and I have to take him to the dentist. Next day, and it's 'roughhousing boys, an accident, Parker already apologized.' Bell cries through an entire call with his dad because he says

Parker is teasing him again, and you say Parker was just trying to be funny; it's Bell who misinterpreted it. Now my son and his friends drive their pride and joy, a massive project they spent months on, straight through your party, ruining it and throwing away any chance of competing in a contest that was all they could talk about, and you're saying they did it for no reason? Come on! At what point are you going to open your eyes? Your kid is a bully, and he pushed too far!"

Mr. Hellickson's face was all twisted up like a Halloween mask. Bell sat totally still, the hairs on the back of his neck raised. It was the same for Timmy and Tam.

"Boys," Timmy's mother said softly. "Maybe you should wait outside while we finish this conversation with your principal."

All three shot up as quickly as they could, scampering over one another to get to the waiting room. Before the door closed behind them, they heard Mr. Nguyen say, "Perhaps, given your closeness to the situation, a call to the school superintendent might be helpful . . ."

Seated once more on the carpet, the boys tried to drown out the shouting coming from the office behind them. Timmy even found the same thread he had worried at before and started pulling it again.

"Wish I had my Rubik's Cube," he muttered.

"Would you leave the carpet alone? We're in enough trouble as it is," Tam said.

Bell gazed past them, staring at Mr. Hellickson's door. He couldn't see in, but he could make out shadows.

"I'd do it again," he announced suddenly. "I don't care how much trouble we get in."

"Oh, me too," Timmy said. "No doubt."

Tam looked at both of them. Then he shrugged.

"I guess I would, too."

It took their parents another ten minutes to finish, and when they emerged, none of them seemed pleased. Mr. Hellickson stood in his doorway. Sternly, he informed them that they were all suspended for the next two days, and they wouldn't be allowed to return to Creator Club for the rest of the year. The boys nodded mutely as he laid it all out, and then they shuffled away, their parents guiding them with tight grips on their shoulders. Mr. Hellickson followed them, and Bell could hear him as he stopped at the secretary's desk.

"Have Mrs. Vicker bring Parker Hellickson to my office," he said tersely, and then he turned on his heel and marched back inside.

Bell held his head high as he was escorted to his locker to get his things. It surprised him, what he saw: Teachers shaking their heads or rolling their eyes. Other kids staring and pointing. Parker being forced along by Mrs. Vicker. He shot Bell such a poisonous look that Bell paused in his tracks, but he didn't lower his eyes. Instead, he glanced to his left, where Timmy walked, and to his right, where Tam was still being lectured by his mom. He dared to take a deep breath, no nerves or beans or anything to stop him.

As soon as he got home, Bell's mom made him write up a list of chores. At the top of the list was calling Mr. Randolph to apologize for getting kicked out of Creator Club. It took Bell most of the day to get through, but right around dinnertime, his teacher picked up.

"I accept your apology," Mr. Randolph said once Bell finished.

"You're not mad?"

"Young man, my tenure in this profession would be short-lived indeed if I got mad every time a student made a mistake."

Bell sighed with relief.

"Doesn't mean I'm not disappointed, though. I took a look at that tank after your driving debacle. It was a work of art."

"Thanks . . ."

"Which you elected to use as a battering ram."

Bell scratched at his cheek. "That was kind of an accident."

"And who do you think had to clean up afterward?"

"Um . . . Mr. Hellickson?"

"Heck no! Like I'm going to let that man drag a perfect re-creation of da Vinci's tank to the curb for some garbage truck to haul away?"

"You took it?"

"Darn right I did," Mr. Randolph said. "It's sitting in my workshop at the university as we speak."

"What are you going to do with it?"

"Me? Nothing, except maybe yank some of my lazy grad students in to show them how a bunch of elementary school kids are outclassing them. No, it's what you're going to do with it that's important. I called and talked to your mother last night. When the school year is over, all three of you mischief-makers are coming in to repair the damage to the hull, maybe get some of those feathers out of the gearworks. Then we're donating it to the children's museum."

Bell smiled. "That seems fair."

"More than fair. It's just. And it's the only way I'm letting you back into Creator Club next year."

"Yes, sir," Bell said.

"Good night, Bell."

"'Night, Mr. Randolph."

Bell started to put the phone down, but a glance at the time made him think of one more call he wanted to make. He looked up her number in the online directory, sat down at the table, and dialed Daelynn.

"How bad?" she whispered after they exchanged hellos.

"Suspended for two days," he replied.

"Harsh!"

"I guess. My mom already has a three-page list of things I'm going to have to work on."

"Is there any way I can help? I was in on it, too, after all."

"Actually," Bell said. "Yes. Can you come over on Saturday? We're going to be rebuilding Mr. Hellickson's flatbed."

"You can do that?"

Bell laughed. "I think so."

"And can I bring Ashi?"

Bell shrugged. "Sure."

"I'll check with my parents, then."

"Cool. But that's not why I'm calling . . ."

"One sec," Daelynn said. He heard her dad shouting something in the distance and Daelynn begging for a few more minutes. Whatever he replied made her giggle. Bell grinned.

"I'm sorry," she said. "You were saying something?"

"I just wanted to know how your day went. With all of us gone, I was worried that Parker might have . . ."

"Oh, you didn't hear?" Daelynn whispered excitedly. Bell could tell she was holding her hand over her mouth to keep her parents from hearing. "Parker, Justin, and Shipman got called to the principal's office right after you. I guess they must have admitted to destroying our balloon, because they were all suspended for the rest of the week! You'll be back before them!"

Bell exhaled. "So you're safe."

"We all are, thanks to your system . . . and that wild stunt! You guys rolled that thing down the street, slammed into Parker's float, then popped out wearing pillows and goggles, and everybody calls *me* weird?"

"Well . . ."

"Look, all I'm saying is it makes a huge difference, having people looking out for me. And having other people to look out for."

"Totally. I'm . . . I'm really glad you moved here, Daelynn."

There was a pause. Bell wished he could see her reaction.

"I'm not going to lie. I'm never going to forget Oregon, and my horses, and my friends. I miss them terribly, every day. But, Bell?"

"Yeah?"

"Today at school, when you weren't there? I missed you, too."

Bell blushed. "Thanks. I'll see you Wednesday."

"Oh! One more thing, Bell!"

"Yeah?"

"Your dad's puzzle . . . I worked on it more over the weekend. I think I might have found a way . . ."

EPILOGUE

Servicechat.Army.Gov

😊 What's up, Bell?

Connected

🔔 Hey, Dad.

🔔 *Image Uploading*

🔔 *Image Uploaded*

😊 Sweet.

🔔 Is it right?

😊 Do you want it to be right?

Dad . . .

Pretty cool how all those pieces fit together in unexpected ways, eh?

Yeah, actually.

That's one of my favorite parts of being an engineer.

Mine, too.

Love you, Bell. See you tomorrow.

I can't wait ☺.

ACKNOWLEDGMENTS

The predicament Bell deals with in this novel is one I found myself in when I was a kid. It took me a while to drum up the courage to write about it, just like it took me years to break free from the roles of victim and bystander. In both cases, I couldn't have succeeded without help. Much as with Bell, that help came in the form of finding the people who would ultimately accept me as I was. Time and distance have, in some cases, seen us drift apart, but I'd like to take a moment to thank them nonetheless, because it was their generosity of spirit, their kindness, and their friendship which transformed my middle school experience. Greg, Luke, and Tiffany; Ben, Davids (T. and M.), and Elisabeth; Joe, Lucy, and Stephanie; Chris, Jim, and Holly—thank you. You taught me how to be a good friend, and as a result I've made many more. Y'all are my Timmy, Tam, and Daelynn.

You'd think that I wouldn't need to do as much research for a book set in the town where I grew up, based loosely on events I lived. That, though, is precisely the reason I had to brush up on the details—I wanted to get this right. To do so required yet more help, and for it I'm grateful. Thank you to Evan Shaw and the faculty and students of Wyoming Middle School for welcoming me back and giving me a tour of the new construction (especially the Woodside Fab L.A.B.!).

Thanks, too, to Lucy Nguyen for your help with names and background details. My appreciation goes to the curators and staff at the Connecticut Science Center for hosting the fantastic Leonardo da Vinci exhibit, including the life-sized recreation of da Vinci's tank. It proved most inspirational! And to the sharp minds of the class of '96, whose recollections of our float-building triumphs and tragedies were an essential trip down memory lane.

On the craft side, I owe much, as always, to the team at Feiwel and Friends: my spectacular editor, Liz Szabla, who encouraged me to dig into Daelynn's background (I love what I found there!); Amanda Mustafic and Morgan Rath in publicity; Rich Deas and the art department; and all the other wonderful book people at Macmillan that do so much to get my stories into readers' hands. And to Rebecca Stead, my agent, my *sine qua non*—it continues to be my honor and privilege to work with you and learn from you.

Kudos for the refinement of this story belong to my team of dedicated second readers, who aren't afraid to give me the feedback every author needs: Adam Solomon, Jennifer Shaw, Caroline Huber and the Simon/Huber family, Annette Ellis, Jennifer Friedman, Jim Adams, Donald Burt, and Ruthann and Theodore Gill. You read, you listened, and you responded. Thank you.

Finally, and as always, thanks to my forever people: Elizabeth, Lauriann, and Lyra. I love you.